"Allie? There are a million reasons I shouldn't touch you."

"Yeah," she said a bit sharply. "Naturally. Hale Scribner, the man who won't let anyone close. God forbid a mere woman should penetrate your armor."

"Hell, you're not a mere woman. I've told you things I've never told anyone else."

"So. Just save your precious isolation and go away."

Quite to the contrary, he leaned over her, caught her chin gently in his hand and turned her face upward so he could kiss her. No light brushing, but a strong, determined kiss.

"Allie," he breathed. "I want you. I want all your fire, all your stubbornness, all your fear and bravery. You take my breath away."

She wanted a snappy comeback, but it wasn't there. Instead, her arm, as if it had a mind of its own, reached up to wrap around his powerful shoulders.

"Are you sure?" he asked against her lips, his breath a warm whisper.

"Yes." A quiet reply.

"Then I'd better get rid of this holster."

CONARD COUNTY: CHRISTMAS BODYGUARD

New York Times Bestselling Author

RACHEL LEE

HARLEQUIN
INTRIGUE

HARLEQUIN®
INTRIGUE®

Recycling programs
for this product may
not exist in your area.

ISBN-13: 978-1-335-48926-5

Conard County: Christmas Bodyguard

Copyright © 2021 by Susan Civil-Brown

This edition published by arrangement with Harlequin Books S.A.

For questions and comments about the quality of this book,
please contact us at CustomerService@Harlequin.com.

Harlequin Enterprises ULC
22 Adelaide St. West, 40th Floor
Toronto, Ontario M5H 4E3, Canada
www.Harlequin.com

Printed in U.S.A.

Rachel Lee was hooked on writing by the age of twelve and practiced her craft as she moved from place to place all over the United States. This *New York Times* bestselling author now resides in Florida and has the joy of writing full-time.

Books by Rachel Lee

Harlequin Intrigue

Conard County: The Next Generation

Cornered in Conard County
Missing in Conard County
Murdered in Conard County
Conard County Justice
Conard County: Hard Proof
Conard County: Traces of Murder
Conard County: Christmas Bodyguard

Harlequin Romantic Suspense

Conard County: The Next Generation

Undercover Hunter
Playing with Fire
Conard County Witness
A Secret in Conard County
A Conard County Spy
Conard County Marine
Undercover in Conard County
Conard County Revenge
Conard County Watch
Stalked in Conard County

Visit the Author Profile page at Harlequin.com.

CAST OF CHARACTERS

Allie Burton—Accountant on the run from a tycoon with multinational connections. He has threatened her.

Hale Scribner—Allie's bodyguard, who owns a private security company. Military background.

Detective Max Roles—Allie's adopted uncle, who is investigating the tycoon and tells Allie to hire Hale and go on the run.

Jasper Ellis—The tycoon who lets no one get in his way and makes troublesome people "disappear."

Stu—Hale Scribner's chief of intelligence.

Chapter One

"You need a bodyguard."

Allie Burton's jaw dropped as soon as her dad's old friend, Detective Max Roles, spoke the words.

It took a few beats for Allie to reply. "Oh, come on, Max. That's over the top. I'm sure Mr. Ellis was talking about all his international businesses, about protecting his companies. He said he'd put the auditing firm on it."

Max was getting up in years. His jowls made him look like a bloodhound with a bald head. Allie had known him all her life, thanks to his friendship with her father, who had died years ago. She trusted him, but this?

"What were his *exact* words, Allie?"

She pulled them up from recent memory. She'd mentioned it lightly to Max, but he wasn't taking it lightly.

"He said, *exactly*, that I shouldn't tell anyone anything about what I'd found in the books."

Max shook his head. "And the rest?"

She shrugged. "He said, and I quote, *Bad things can happen*. Well, of course they could. He's a tycoon with companies all over the world. Any irregularity in the books could cause big problems."

"Right," Max said. He sipped on his perpetual coffee. "I want you to think about that. Bad things can happen."

"Well…"

"Don't 'well' me. Just listen."

Allie frowned. "I guess you're one of the people I shouldn't have told about this. I thought you'd laugh and wouldn't tell anyone."

"I won't tell anyone except the bodyguard you're going to hire."

"Damn, Max. How am I supposed to afford that anyway?"

Max shook his head again. "Your grandfather left you a pile, didn't he?"

Allie rolled her eyes. "And I'm supposed to waste it on this?"

"It's not wasted if it saves your life," Max said sharply. "Now will you just listen, or are you going to be like my damn dog who only listens when he feels like it?"

Allie could have smirked at the thought of Max's stubborn mastiff, a dog bigger than Max, but she resisted the urge. Folding her hands primly in her lap, she gave in. "I'm listening."

"About damn time." Max reached for his cigarettes, a habit Allie often tried to get him to break. She pointedly waved smoke away.

"Cut it out," he said mildly. "You won't get cancer from half an hour."

She sighed. "Just tell me what you think I need to know."

"Gladly. Or unhappily. You've been on the inside of Jasper Ellis's business. You know he's like an octopus with a whole lot of tentacles."

"He's successful. So what?"

Max leaned forward. "I have nothing against the man's success. One of the things I can tell you is we've been investigating him for years, and we've never found a thing we could hang on him. He's good at covering evidence. Hell, he's better than good. The government could take lessons from him. Not that his methods would be legal."

"Investigating him for what?"

Max blew a cloud. "For the unexplained disappearances and supposed suicides of a number of his employees."

Allie felt a chill run down her spine. She could tell that Max wasn't joking. Her own dismissal of the situation began to feel naïve. "You're kidding," she murmured.

"I wish I was. Here's the thing. At first it could be dismissed. But then the numbers really caught our attention and we started looking into it. Nothing traces directly back to Ellis except he's at the top of the pyramid. Or the head on the octopus, to round out my original analogy. You may remember I fought against you going to work for him."

Allie did. Max had strenuously argued with her, something he never did. He was doing it right now.

That worried her as much as what he was saying because Max believed it.

He was not a man given to conspiracy theories. A hard-nosed detective, he stuck to the facts. He seemed to have some facts right now.

"Allie, the cops can't protect you. We wouldn't have justification since his threat was so indirect. But you tweaked the tiger's tail, evidently with something that he needs to hide. Jasper Ellis is not a man to cross."

Allie's voice was growing thin. "I only told him so he could fix it. So there'd be no trouble for him or his businesses."

"Does he care? You have knowledge that could harm him. He takes care of those threats. Somehow."

Forgetting the perfect posture her aunt had drilled into her, Allie slumped back in the chair. "Really, Max?"

"Really. So I'm going to call that bodyguard. I've known him for years since he was still in the Marines. I trust him with your life. And you're not leaving my house before he gets here."

"God, Max!"

"Just go make yourself a cup of whatever. Or have some orange juice. But you are *not* going anywhere."

He punctuated those words like bullet shots. Truly shaken, Allie rose to get that orange juice. Could this possibly be true? But she trusted Max. Completely. He'd been like an uncle to her for most of her life. If Max said it, it was true.

As she passed through the short hallway, she saw her reflection in the full-length mirror. Max's wife had placed it there years ago, before she had passed from a stray gunshot.

Allie paused, staring at her reflection, wondering who that woman in there was. She felt so changed that she shouldn't look the same. Neat dark blue business slack suit, a blue striped button-down shirt, collar open. Her ash-blond hair in a fluffed loose short cut because she didn't feel like fussing with it. A trim every couple of weeks solved that problem.

A bodyguard? The thought sent a tendril of ice creeping along her spine. Seriously?

Before she continued along the hall, Max called to her. "Get that frozen key lime pie out, will you? Never met anybody who didn't like it. Hale will be here in about an hour and it takes that long to thaw."

The juxtaposition of a threat and a key lime pie seemed absurd. Except she couldn't smile at it or laugh about it. Her face had grown as frozen as her spine. "Sure," she called back, glad that her voice didn't shake while everything inside her felt as if an earthquake had begun.

She pulled the pie from its box and left it covered on the counter to thaw. Then, deciding she couldn't possibly swallow orange juice, she returned to the small living room with empty hands.

She asked, "You really think I'm in danger?" The war inside her still had not quit.

"Jasper Ellis is not a man I'd want to screw with."

"But if I don't tell anyone…"

Max repeated himself slowly, firmly. "You have dangerous knowledge. He only wants you to keep your mouth shut until he can deal with you."

Allie's world was tilting off its axis. She vaguely wondered if life would ever appear the same again. If life would ever *be* the same again. A whole new reality bore down on her and she hated it.

Her wonderful Max was about to entertain a bodyguard with pie. Seriously?

"For heaven's sake, Max…" *For heaven's sake what? Fix my world for me?*

"I know," he said. "It's a shock. Kinda like the first murder scene a cop goes to. Nothing's ever the same again."

Max fell silent, lighting another cigarette. This time Allie didn't make a show of waving away the smoke. What harm could it do her if her life was truly threatened?

"God," she muttered. "I can't believe this." But she did. Max's words had pierced her like an arrow. An internal ache began, twisting her stomach painfully.

"Just listen to Hale," Max said presently. "He's tuned in. He'll know."

Allie could only stare at him. Belief still warred with the conviction that this was impossible. "Mr. Ellis could fix the problem I found."

"He could. But consider that the man has been under constant IRS audit and they still haven't nailed him. You might well have found the irregularity that could blow the whole thing open."

She hadn't considered that. She could scarcely imagine the back taxes and penalties that might ensue. It would damage the share price, costing him additional wealth. Or worse.

"God," she whispered again.

Max let her ruminate in silence.

She could just get up and walk out of here now. Continue at work tomorrow as if nothing had happened. Except it had. Max was right about that.

The protection guy arrived a bit earlier than projected. When Max opened the door, the first thing Allie noticed was his height. Wearing a loose windbreaker and jeans, he didn't appear muscular, but that probably wasn't necessary for what he did.

At least he didn't appear muscular until he greeted Max, stepped inside and twisted to look at Allie. As the windbreaker moved, it outlined wide shoulders and powerful arms. In shape.

First impressions and all that. Okay, he was intimidating and trying to conceal it. His face was as impassive as rock, some of it hidden behind a scraggly beard. His hair was long and shaggy, nearly inky. Eye color indeterminate in the inside lighting although it, too, appeared dark. In all, not very reputable in appearance.

Max made the introductions. "Alicia Burton, Hale Scribner. Take a seat, Hale. Allie's run into a problem with Jasper Ellis."

Both of Hale's eyebrows lifted as he settled onto an edge of the couch, the only place remaining with Max in his favorite, battered recliner. He splayed his denim-clad legs and rested his elbows on them. Allie already perched on a gooseneck chair. All the upholstery was dark in color. It probably concealed a lot of spills from over the years.

Hale spoke, his voice deep and carrying something like darkness. "Jasper Ellis, huh? How much trouble?"

Max replied. "He said bad things can happen."

Now the great stone face darkened. "Not good."

"Which is what I keep trying to get Allie to believe. I can understand why she's finding it so difficult."

Hale nodded, a sharp movement of his head. "Jasper Ellis is bad news. Very bad news."

The chill dripped down Allie's spine again. "You both really think he'd kill me?"

Hale answered, his voice calm and steady. "Absolutely. You wouldn't be the first."

Allie gave up. She put her head in her hand. "God, Max."

"She's not going to help. Ellis sold his soul a long time ago."

Allie had always liked the way Max referred to God as *she*. Turned out that was okay in their Catholic religion. She'd checked the first time he'd used the gender. But that didn't help at all.

Hale remained silent. Allie looked at him again, finding nothing reassuring in his nearly immovable face.

She spoke. "So what do you do? Keep an eye on me in my apartment?"

"No."

The single word was unilluminating. "What, then?" she demanded.

"You're going to leave that apartment. I'd need a whole phalanx of guards to protect you, and there'd still be a way to get to you. Even the best group is permeable."

Allie's insides tightened again, enhancing the ache that was already there. "Then what?"

Max spoke. "How about we have some key lime pie, then discuss this in more detail."

Max was not to be deterred. He disappeared into the kitchen and returned with three white pie plates, each decorated with a fork and a wedge of pie. He passed them around.

"Eat," he said. "Food always helps."

Allie doubted anything would help, but she obediently took a small mouthful of pie. Hale was not so delicate. Clearly he was a man who enjoyed his food.

Allie still waited for answers.

At last Hale set aside his plate on the end table and wiped his fingers and mouth with a napkin. Finally he settled his attention on Allie.

"We're going on the run."

Now her stomach dropped and her brain sought a way to deny what he was suggesting. "Isn't that overkill? Run how far?"

"As far as it takes until I can find Ellis's goons. Until I can be sure you're safe."

"Oh, come on," Allie retorted, feeling stubbornness rise in her. "That's not necessary."

"It is if you want to be alive in a week."

Allie could no longer contain her growing anxiety. Her stomach twisted until she wanted to vomit. Her breath came raggedly, fast.

"Put your head down," Max said amiably. "If that doesn't work I'll get you a paper bag."

Why did she have the feeling that he wasn't as distressed by this as she was, then realized, *because Max*. He never let anything disturb him too much. Maybe to help her calm down.

At last she was able to lift her head, her breathing stabilizing even if her stomach didn't.

"I don't understand all of this," she said weakly. "I don't. He didn't threaten me."

Hale spoke. "He did. I've heard enough indirect threats to recognize one. I also know enough about Ellis. Max isn't exaggerating. We go on the run."

A nice dark hole sounded good right then. A cave. A storm drain. She wasn't feeling picky.

"What good will that do?"

Hale answered. "It'll keep you out of the line of fire until I can take care of the threat."

"How can you do that if you're running with me?"

"I have contacts."

As if that explained anything. Maybe it did. She was having trouble wrapping her mind around all this. She wanted more in the way of explanations, but suspected she wasn't going to get it. She looked at Max.

"Do it, Allie," he said. "I love you. Just do it for me."

That was a plea she couldn't ignore. Again she looked at Hale. "How do we do this?"

"First we go to your bank and withdraw enough cash to cover my retainer and our expenses. Cash can't be traced."

Her stomach lurched. "And then?"

"I'm taking you back to your apartment. I'll give you a couple of duffels, easier to manage than suitcases. You'll pack for a time in rough areas. Like you're going camping. None of those business suits."

Her stomach rolled again. If Max thought this was good, safe, she would do it. "After that?"

"Then we're getting the hell out of this city. First night out you're going to dye your hair. Then we move again."

"Oh, God," she whispered. Appalled. A nightmare was descending.

Hale rose. "Don't call your friends. Don't tell them you'll be away. Leave no hint of our plans." He looked at the impressive black watch on his wrist. "We go to the bank first. They'll still be open. Apartment next. Then we leave. Together."

He gave her one last look. "Ellis probably thinks he has a few days. You went to work today, right?"

She nodded.

"Then he probably thinks you don't suspect anything yet. We'll get going because tomorrow morning he'll know you've slipped the noose." He paused. "Wait here. I have some friends I need to speak with."

HALE MET HIS best buddy at a small out-of-the-way coffee shop. Stu Dembrowski had fought beside him and worked beside him since Afghanistan. They'd each saved the other's life, and a deep trust had grown between them. More trust than Hale could usually muster.

"Jasper Ellis," he said to Stu.

"Oh, man, you're not going up against *him*!"

"I need to. And what I need from you and the rest of the crew is tracking devices. Get them on as many cars from Ellis's local security team as you can. If necessary, follow some of them on the road until you get an opportunity to tag them. Then I'm going to call in frequently for position reports."

Stu nodded. "And you'll be where?"

"Driving all over like a maniac. Can do?"

"Will do," Stu answered firmly. "Just remember, those transmitters don't work everywhere. There'll be some gaps."

"I can still get enough information to put it together."

Stu nodded and rose. "We'll get to work."

Hale waited five minutes before leaving the coffee shop. Then he followed a circuitous route back to Max and Alicia Burton.

There wasn't any time to waste.

Chapter Two

Hale followed Allie to the bank as he'd said he would. The huge sum he wanted her to withdraw made her catch her breath.

"You'll have to sign some kind of papers for the IRS," he warned her. "Just do it."

She did this while he waited outside with a black duffel for her. She practically had to swear to the bank officer that she knew what she was doing. Then she signed all the paperwork, and twenty minutes later walked out with a very large bank bag containing small denominations of an unbelievable sum of money.

Hale stepped into the outer lobby and opened the duffel. She dropped the heavy bank bag in it.

"Now to your apartment."

Allie drove her car, her hands shaking, and hoped she didn't have an accident. Well, that was one way to kill her.

She made it into the parking garage. Hale was right behind in his massive black Suburban, pulling into a guest slot. As promised, he carried several duffel bags as he followed her into the elevator.

For the first time she wondered if he was armed. If so, it wasn't showing under his windbreaker.

Rather rudely, she thought, he supervised her packing. She wasn't overloaded with jeans or sweatshirts or heavy jackets. Or anything really. She mostly limited herself to summery weekend hikes with friends. Some lazing-around clothes.

"Bring just a few days of underwear," he told her. "We can pick up other clothes for you along the way."

With the untraceable cash, she supposed. Maybe the best thing to do would be to pretend she was starring in a suspense movie. For now. Just pretend and get this part over.

"Leave your cell phone behind," he ordered. "It can be tracked and there's no way to prevent it even if you turn it off. Every cell tower we pass will ping you."

Leave her phone? It would be like cutting off her arm. She wasted a few minutes and he waited while she deleted apps such as her bank.

"My friends will notice I'm gone."

He answered. "I'm sure they will, but you don't want to draw them into this mess. I'll arrange for you to call them in a few days."

Hale carried her bags and threw them in the back of the Suburban. He waved her into the passenger seat, then they were driving away. Away from her life as she knew it.

Sickened again, all she could do was look out the darkly tinted windows at the passing familiarity of her neighborhood. Then she closed her eyes, trying not to care anymore.

Hale never spoke a word.

ALLIE MUST HAVE fallen asleep, amazingly enough, because when she next looked out at the world, night had fallen and they had driven into the spreading suburbs. Traffic on the highway had lightened from its usual rush-hour crunch. Hale drove near the top of the speed limit.

"We'll stop when we get out of this mess and get something to eat," he said, speaking for the first time since they left. "You must be getting hungry by now."

"I don't know if I'll ever want to eat again."

"Think of it as survival."

Allie apparently needed to think in those terms now. Horrifying. "Do we have to travel like this?"

"Trust me to know my job."

No conversation. She got it. Well, no entertainment there. "Radio?"

"Lady, I ripped off everything on this truck that could be traced by anyone. No friendly voice giving me directions or asking me what kind of music or who I want to call."

She figured she would come to hate this man before long. "So nothing?"

"I didn't even leave the radio. Taking no chances. You never know what technology can do these days. Maybe along the way we'll find some CDs you like."

Like she was going to be shopping for CDs during this awful trek. She smothered a sigh, fearing it might be audible over the quietly purring engine. "It's almost Christmas," she remarked irrelevantly.

"I heard."

End of subject. Allie wasn't accustomed to sitting

around with nothing to do. If friends didn't come over or call, she had music, she had books, she had cooking. Now she had nothing except this taciturn man who obviously wasn't going to provide much in the way of distraction.

Max, what did you get me into?

Several hours later, when houses and people had dissipated to almost nothing, he pulled over at a gas station with a diner beside it. Oh, man, the best food in the world, she thought sarcastically. Fat and more fat. Overcooked veggies that might have come out of a can.

"Stay in the car while I gas up," Hale told her. "Then we'll find you a bathroom and food."

The bathroom would probably be awful. She gave up her internal struggle. Whatever else happened, she was here for now.

To her amazement, Hale didn't follow her into the bathroom, and the bathroom sparkled. Somebody cared. The tables and booths were clean, too, and the menu made a stab at catering to urban tastes.

"Eat more than a salad," Hale ordered her. "We may not see food again until tomorrow."

Planning ahead, she thought, but for once she didn't get stubborn. What was the point? She heeded him. Besides, this gave her an opportunity to eat foods she liked but normally avoided because they weren't healthful.

A hamburger and fries with a side of salad. When was the last time she'd eaten fries and a burger? And this proved to be good food. Tasty. She decided to enjoy her excuse.

Hale ate in silence. Surprise. Not. He had two burgers, a double portion of fries and some onion rings.

He apparently felt this diner with its short-order cook and two waitresses would keep her safe enough for twenty minutes while he took his own bathroom break. Then he threw cash on the table, and insisted she head for the locked SUV. He followed at a distance, probably keeping an eye out.

Once they were on the road again, she spoke. "I bet you don't come cheap."

"Not since I was in the Marines. Worried about my retainer?"

"Just curious."

"You ought to be. Twenty grand."

Ouch. "You definitely aren't cheap."

"For this you don't want cheap."

He had a point. "Max seemed awfully sure about you. He didn't call anyone else."

"Max and I go back a ways. I've done jobs for him before."

Allie wondered what kind of jobs but figured he wouldn't tell her. Nor should he, she guessed. She'd want her own privacy.

She tried to settle more comfortably into her seat and resign herself to this road trip continuing for a while.

As HALE WATCHED his Suburban eat up miles of highway, some of it winding away from major arteries and into narrower roads through small towns, he decided Allie Burton might be a handful.

He felt nearly constant resistance in her, even when

she didn't argue or protest. Eventually some of that was going to burst out of her. Not everyone could be like his previous protectees, terrified and willing to do anything.

Maybe the seriousness of this threat hadn't really sunk in yet. He'd find out, he supposed.

He needed to find a pharmacy or retail store to get her the hair dye. Her ash-blond hair was striking, striking enough to be noticed.

But Jasper Ellis. The idea that Allie was in trouble with that man seriously worried Hale. He knew Ellis's reputation, knew how concerned the police were, and knew from his web of contacts that the body count was getting high.

Now, for the first time, he had someone to protect from Ellis. He didn't think it was going to be easy. Hale had a small business, relying a lot on friends who knew how to glean intelligence. He didn't begin to have Ellis's resources. Not even remotely.

But he also knew his own capabilities.

First he had to get Allie far enough away, surreptitiously enough, that she'd be somewhat protected from whomever Ellis sent after her. Then he could deal with *that* threat and maybe gather information that would help the cops get Ellis. There was no other way to keep Allie Burton safe long-term.

This was an unusual case for him. Most people he protected suffered from a single personal threat. Allie was a whole new ball game.

And he didn't doubt that at some point in this flight

she was going to dig her heels in. He just hoped it didn't come too soon.

That first night he booked them into an out-of-the-way seedy motel. Not what she was accustomed to, he was certain.

He had phony IDs and checked them in himself, paying in cash. Allie glumly watched the entire process. Her money, being used for this.

"Retail store or pharmacy nearby?" Hale asked the clerk when he received the keys.

"Up the road about half a mile. Small grocery, good enough. Has nearly everything we need around here."

Hale hoped that included hair dye. He expected a struggle from Allie over that. He was not to be disappointed.

But first he insisted she remain in the locked car while he went in to find the dye. Trying to avoid notice, he added a few bottles of water and some small snack items to his purchase. The kinds of things most travelers might buy.

When he climbed back into his car, he sensed annoyance once again. Well, he'd be pretty annoyed himself at having everything taken out of his hands.

Small talk had never been his thing. Since he'd never practiced it, he didn't know how to make it. Less said the better.

But Allie must feel like a lump on the seat beside him. He spared some thought on figuring out what he might say but was soon relieved of the necessity by the return to the motel.

He left all the bags in the car, taking only the hair dye. They wouldn't be here for long, anyway.

He could hardly wait to hear her reaction, first to the dye, then to the news they'd be moving again tonight.

As he expected, she looked at the box of dye he handed her and said, "No way."

"You have distinctive hair."

"I *like* it."

He reached into his well of patience. "I understand why. It's very pretty. It also makes you easier to recognize. You'll have to resign yourself to this."

Her response was a mulish look, but after a minute she headed to the bathroom. "Are you immovable?" she demanded over her shoulder.

"When it's best. If you need help with that stuff, let me know."

LIKE ALLIE WANTED his hands all over her head. No way. She pulled out the contents of the box, angry enough to tear it a bit, then scanned the directions.

If she needed his help? Did he take her for an idiot? She looked one last time in the mirror, then started the job. Max had recommended him. She must have reminded herself several times as she destroyed her hair.

The woman who looked back at her no longer looked like Allie. All that dark brown hair… She grabbed another towel to dry it off with quick, impatient movements. No comb. Then she looked at the stained towels. Screw it.

When she walked back to the other room, doing her

best to finger comb her fluffy cut, Hale said, "Much better."

"I beg to differ."

He nodded. "You would. Let's go."

Her jaw dropped for the second time that day. "Go where?"

"Get on the road."

She felt her face settle into stubborn lines. "Why the hell? You checked us in for the night."

"And we were in this town too long. I went into that grocery. Time to kick the dust off our heels."

"Oh, for Pete's sake. Hale, you're out of your mind."

"I know my job. Let's go."

She studied the immovable monolith that was Hale Scribner and tried to tell herself he knew what he was doing. He was right, it was his job. That didn't mean she had to like it.

"Damn," was all she said and headed for the door. "After this is over, I'm going to find a way to get even with you."

He didn't answer. She no longer expected it. Although he'd already explained why they had to move on, they hadn't been here that long and it seemed unlikely to her that anyone would notice them.

He was paranoid, she thought grimly as she climbed into his SUV. Paranoid as hell.

But that seemed to be part of his job, too.

Chapter Three

Miles of country road fell away behind them. Wiggling like a snake, this way and that, Hale was always keeping an eye out for a tail. Nothing yet.

They had until morning to get as far away as possible. As soon as Ellis or one of his minions realized Allie hadn't come to work and wasn't answering her phone, the hunt would begin—if it hadn't already.

Hale said nothing as Allie fell asleep beside him. She must be exhausted after such a stressful day, but when she awoke she was bound to pepper him with questions. Rightfully so, since the only reason she feared Ellis was because of Max.

God help her if she hadn't had such a good friend.

The eastern sky had just begun to lighten with a hazy red when Allie stirred.

"Dang," she muttered sleepily, "I don't think I can take another minute in this seat. I ache all over."

"I'm not surprised. Hang in there for a bit longer. There's a rest area a few miles ahead, amazingly enough considering we're on a back road."

She stirred again and sat up higher, looking around them. "Where are we?"

"In the middle of nowhere."

"Well, that sounds inviting." Her answer was sarcastic.

In a way, he agreed with her. Other than the fact that they were getting into the mountains of Northern California, which were beautiful. Ahead, Mount Shasta's perennial snowcap burned with the sun's early glow. At least the glaciers hadn't melted, not completely. Rolling land surrounded them.

"*Why* are we here?"

"How well do you know Jasper Ellis?"

She sighed. "He seems like a nice enough man. Not at all threatening."

"He wouldn't." Hale paused, turning them onto a different road, this one heading east. "He wouldn't have made it this far if anyone thought he was a villain."

A minute of silence from her. "I guess so. But why are you and Max both so certain he's dangerous?"

Hale pondered how best to answer that question, given that there was no evidence. He put words together because sometimes he couldn't choose reticence.

"Because," he said slowly, "too many people who work for him have disappeared or died by suicide. More than can be explained by statistical averages." He figured she'd understand that because she was an accountant. She worked with numbers all the time.

Naturally she had an answer. "But statistics can only show correlation unless the numbers are high enough."

"The numbers are high enough that the police have been investigating for years."

That hushed her, but not for very long. "How can anyone be certain Ellis is behind it?"

"As tight a grip as he keeps? Because no one would dare do any of this without his approval. Too much risk."

Then, after a few minutes, Allie asked, "What are we doing?"

"Ellis will figure out you've taken a runner shortly after you haven't come to work. When they can't call you to find out what's wrong."

"That still doesn't explain this."

"Actually it does. I need to get you as far away as I can before he sends someone out to find you. I have to make us untraceable." Unless someone had managed to put a tracker on his car. He couldn't imagine how, though, as fast as they'd moved. He'd check soon anyway. For now he didn't mind the possibility because it might reassure Ellis's men that they could find Allie. Might make them slower.

"So that's why we're in the middle of nowhere."

"Exactly." Mount Shasta's glow was becoming brighter, whiter.

"I couldn't have remained in the city?"

He paused, turning them another way. "Funny thing about cities. They seem anonymous but you'd probably be surprised to learn how many people you've met, people who would recognize you, at least from a photo. Everyone from restaurant waiters to places you go regularly, like a jogging trail or a park. Where you shop. Where you go to a doctor or dentist. That's why the witness protection plan moves people hundreds of miles away."

Silence claimed her again briefly. "I need a bathroom."

"A few more miles unless you want the side of the road."

Apparently not, because she didn't speak again. At last he found the rest area. It was small, probably not very well-kept, but nature's call and all that.

He felt they were safe enough to allow her to go by herself. A vending machine offered a selection of canned drinks and junk food. It would have to do for now.

When she emerged, he asked her what she wanted. "It'll be a while before I can get us a meal."

She nodded, her fight gone for now. It would come back.

"This looks awful except for the canned cranberry juice."

"Pick something anyway. You need food before you're up to arguing with me again."

She sent a startled glance his way, then smiled faintly before choosing some chips and a candy bar. He made sure to get her several cans of cranberry juice. She'd want them later, if not now.

He wondered if she had any idea how very pretty she was. How memorable. Probably. Most attractive women did. He allowed her nearly ten minutes to walk around and stretch. He did the same, keeping a weather eye out for any car that slowed down as it passed.

Then the road again.

"I need a shower."

"Today, I promise. I could use one, too, before you're hanging out the car window to avoid smelling me."

That at least got a small laugh out of her.

ALLIE SETTLED BACK into the rhythm of the road, not at all happy about any of this. The seat beneath her felt more comfortable than it had upon awakening, but that was small by comparison with this insane trip.

It was like being kidnapped, she thought. She didn't even know where she was. Max had put the kibosh on those fears, however. Max wanted this, and Hale appeared to know what he was doing.

At least he'd explained, although not nearly enough. She was still having trouble believing that Jasper Ellis could be the evil they said he was.

But thinking back over the nearly two years she had worked for the man, she had to admit she'd heard whispers. She'd always dismissed them because rumors were so unreliable and often fanciful.

Maybe not. In the brightening land of Northern California, with Mount Shasta as a guidepost, she at least had some vague idea of their location. Extremely vague. If she were to leap out of the car and try to run, she'd only get lost before she found a phone to call for help.

What if Max and Hale were right?

The man beside her offered only a minimal explanation. Too quiet by half. Her only link to her old life. Her only promise of a safer one.

How the hell was he supposed to find someone sent out to look for her, to put the threat to bed?

But he'd said that was the intention, although she couldn't imagine him managing that. Not if they were hiding as well as he thought.

God, this had turned into a nightmare without any end that she could see. Nor was the taciturn man beside her helping by his decision to say little. It would help if she knew at least a bit about him, but all she knew so far was that he'd been a Marine.

A double helping of frustration for her. She was not accustomed to ceding personal control over her life to someone else. She preferred to make her own decisions. She was also aware that she could be very stubborn about that.

But this time there was Max. She kept coming back to him. He'd managed to unnerve her.

Thus she was riding into the unknown with a monolith of silence. Carved in stone, he seemed.

The restaurant he'd promised turned up two hours later. It advertised "down-home" cooking. She imagined congealed fat.

"Not what you're used to," Hale remarked. "But a good breakfast."

"Have you eaten everywhere on the continent?"

"Hardly."

When? Why? How? She didn't bother to ask, knowing by now that he'd probably ignore her. She zipped her lips and waited for her answers, at least about the food. Soon she was going to demand some answers.

She'd hired the man after all, and she deserved to be some kind of partner in this insanity.

But her life seemed to depend on Hale now. It wouldn't be wise to annoy him too much. At least not yet.

After an onion-and-pepper omelet, cooked by a grill man who was amazing to watch, she felt a whole lot better. She even got to put the marmalade on her own toast, which came without butter at her request. One small victory for independence.

Hale ate a huge breakfast in comparison. Another thing about him that didn't surprise her. Hidden beneath that jacket was a lot of man. He must be ripped.

Eventually they left the diner. This time he didn't allow her to walk around outside. Protecting their secrecy, she supposed. This trip would become tiresome very quickly.

The day had grown overcast, giving her no real sense of the countryside. All she knew was that Mount Shasta had begun to disappear behind them. Then, even that was gone. They headed mostly east now, she guessed. The alternative was driving into the Pacific Ocean.

She loved that ocean, especially north in Oregon. Rugged cliffs standing guard over water that was rough and wave-tossed most of the time. She especially loved those high cliffs. Continental plates colliding. The extreme power of nature visible to the world.

She occasionally indulged a fantasy of living in a house high above the water with a view over the cliffs. Not possible anymore. Oregon protected the coastline, and almost all habitation existed on the shore below. Once fishing villages, she supposed they were now

mostly owned by the wealthy who seemed to be determined to take over every beautiful space on the planet.

She would have enjoyed a drive along that coastline, a lot more than this doglegging trail into the hinterlands. Hours later they'd put away another three or
four hundred miles. Then relief appeared in the form
of a gas station.

She headed for the bathroom and when she emerged
she saw Hale talking on a telephone. She waited until
he finished talking indecipherably in what seemed like
a coded message.

"What is that?" she asked, annoyed because he
hadn't let her bring her own phone.

He held up a finger, quieting her.

Allie bit her lip and waited. Then he walked over
to a huge truck with a business name on the sides and
rear. It appeared to be headed in a different direction.
What the heck?

She watched as he stuck the phone inside a gap in the
truck's rear end, then signaled her to get into the car.
When they were rolling away, he gave her chilling news.

"My contacts say that Ellis is already trying to find
you."

She bit her lip, absorbing the shock. Maybe Ellis was
indeed the man they claimed him to be.

A dozen miles later, she could repress her exaspera-
tion no longer. "You wouldn't let me bring my phone.
Was that a burner of some kind?"

"Not exactly."

She waited for more information and when it didn't

come, she spoke impatiently. "Damn it, Hale. What's not exactly a burner phone?"

He didn't answer immediately. She suspected that he kept telling her only what he felt she needed to know. That irritated her. After all, she was riding passenger on some quest she didn't fully understand.

"Burner phones," he said finally, "aren't exactly burners the way you see them in movies."

"Why not?"

"Because every burner has to be in touch with the service that was paid for and that also provides the location. How else would they know when you exceed your hours? How else would they know when to cut off the service?"

A good point. She looked out the window again, then felt she hadn't been told enough. "What's different about yours?"

He offered a heavy sigh. "Time for some education. I have a whole box of them in the back. A metal box that keeps them from ever being pinged. I bought them all months ago and kept them in there with the batteries removed. After a while the service pings less frequently, then finally not at all, assuming the phone has been lost. They don't bother to cut off the hours then, either."

"I never thought about any of this."

"Why should you?"

"But once you use them…"

"I only use each phone once. Not enough to get any real attention from their algorithms. Then I get rid of it."

"On the back of a truck?" She was growing more astonished by the moment.

"Yes. In case it gets pinged somehow, it'll be pinged moving in the wrong direction. As simple as that."

Now she had plenty to think about. All this secrecy. All this covert activity. All of it to protect her.

Fear began to fill her again. She wanted to be sick.

"I need to pull over," she said, her mouth salivating, her body growing hot.

"Bathroom?"

"I wish."

Her stomach had begun to heave just as he found a place to pull his vehicle to the side of the road. She heard the door lock release when she opened the door. The grass wasn't close enough, but gravel was. At last it stopped.

A rag appeared in front of her face. "It's okay. Just wipe off, then I'm going to give you a swig of water to rinse your mouth. No more than that."

It had to be enough. A lot now was going to have to be enough.

Then they returned to their journey to nowhere.

Chapter Four

Three nights later, the rebellion Hale had been waiting for happened.

He said, "I'm going to an outfitter to get you some more clothes."

Her expression grew stubborn. "Why can't I go with you?"

"For reasons that should be obvious by now. If that hunter has managed to get closer somehow, I don't want him to be able to follow closely with your photo. I told you that. Just give me your sizes."

"You know everything," she said querulously. "I should at least be able to pick out what I wear."

"Not this time."

"Damn it, Hale, we've stayed in a different town in a different motel every single night. We arrive well after dark and leave in the morning before dawn. I doubt even a bloodhound could find us."

He provided a stoic answer. "Of course not. A dog can't track a car indefinitely."

"So why can't I choose my own clothes?"

His face remained expressionless, but she still felt

him studying her as if she were a complex problem. Maybe she was. At least he didn't speak patiently this time, as if to a child.

He was facing her and spoke quietly. "Allie, you'd pick out clothes you like."

"Damn straight."

"That's part of the problem. I don't want you to look anything like you used to. Styles, colors, whatever."

"Oh, God, this is insane. What about the place you buy the clothes? They're not going to notice that a man is buying women's clothes in the wrong size for him?"

"I have a wife," he said flatly, then exited the room, locking the door behind him.

Allie sat down, everything inside her annoyed beyond words, with her unavoidable fear making it worse. She wanted this to end *now*.

He had a wife? She found that hard to believe. Who'd want a silent man like him? Who'd let him run on these long trips without explanation? A woman far more compliant than she, obviously.

Hale returned an hour later, tossing several large bags on the bed. "Change," he ordered. "Everything you brought with you is going into a trash bin farther along the road."

"That's illegal, to use someone else's bin!"

"Most of what I do is illegal. Get used to it. Change, now."

"But…"

"We're leaving as soon as you do."

Again? Wearily she went to do as he demanded. He was right. The clothes he had found for her were nothing she would have chosen for herself. All dull colors. All downscale.

The woman in the mirror had become even more unrecognizable.

When she stepped out, her old clothes wadded in her hand, she found a transformed Hale. His black windbreaker had given way to an army-green jacket with many pockets. While it was open, she saw he wore a double shoulder holster. It didn't shock her. Her father had often worn one when he was in plain clothes on the job. But now she knew why Hale had never removed that windbreaker.

His jeans were the same as before, but his black boots had been replaced by desert boots. Military.

But the biggest transformation was his hair. The shaggy locks were gone, neat now although still a bit long.

"Where'd you get your hair cut?" she demanded.

"I pulled out the extensions. There's a warm jacket in your bags. You might need it. Anything you don't want now I'm throwing in the trunk."

"And my duffels will be empty?"

"Believe it."

Oh, she believed it. Thank God that while her hiking clothes carried famous brand names, they weren't the most expensive items in her wardrobe, not by a long shot. "Just don't throw out my underwear."

"I won't. No one can see it."

Except him, with his hands all over it. Looking at him, she accepted that she wasn't going to win this battle.

Taking his advice, she found the jacket in the bag. A drab match for his. She also discovered a flannel nightgown.

"Oh, for heaven's sake!" As if anyone but him would see her in it. She thought wistfully of the satiny gowns she preferred, even the occasional peignoir. Of the Egyptian-cotton robe for warmth.

No point. Things could all be replaced eventually.

If this nightmare ever ended. Her fear had been slowly subsiding with each day on the road. She was growing so weary of this.

But then fear bit her again, hard. The reality of what was happening with her clothes had just become *real*. The reality of this hardened man sleeping on a floor, giving her no solitude except in a windowless bathroom. It was all *real*.

Max and Hale took the threat seriously. She needed to, as well. Except she hated every moment of this flight.

STUBBORNNESS HAD BEEN replaced by sadness on Allie's face. Hale noticed it before they returned to his car. Noticed it in the inkiness of a night brightened only by a few pale streetlights.

He helped her into her seat this time and received no objection. That was a bad sign indeed. He didn't know what he could possibly do about it.

Pallid streetlights soon gave way to the pitch-black of the road, punctuated only by his headlamps. No other vehicles traveled this way, and Hale allowed himself to relax a bit.

Then the moon started rising to the east, in its quarter phase, yet strong enough to splash the world in blue light. Before long, a wind picked up, tossing the silvery leaves on the trees like ocean waves. A storm was brewing.

The one thing he missed was being able to check the weather on his watch. A watch that had been gutted to its most basic functions. A tool he'd been able to rely on over many years, now merely a possible threat.

Hale didn't like this flight any more than the woman beside him did. He was a man used to confronting danger head-on in one way or another. But this was the career he'd chosen, using his skills to protect the lives of others. It was never glamorous. The only real thanks he got was knowing he'd saved a life.

Even the life of a person he didn't admire at all. Not even a lowlife deserved to be killed. Leaving the law to deal with those clients was better by far.

This one was certainly different. This one was genuinely an innocent. She'd done absolutely nothing to deserve this.

And now she had reached sorrow or despair. He had no way to know which, but either troubled him greatly. Her life had been changed by trying to be a good person. She would never see the world through the same eyes again. The man who initiated this needed to spend the rest of his days in jail, stripped of the power he worshipped and the money he loved.

And, damn it, he was going to find a way to ensure that. To ensure that Allie didn't need to live the rest of her life in fear.

But how? The question haunted him.

ALLIE HAD DOZED but now she woke to the suffocating cocoon of darkness. She'd slept her way through so much of this trip that she wondered if she'd ever be able to sleep through the night again.

A bolt of lightning ripped the sky, blinding in its brilliance. So fast it offered little illumination.

"A storm," she murmured pointlessly.

"I was hoping we'd outrun it, but maybe not."

"Not likely, given that you're driving to every point of the compass and a few that I'm sure don't exist." Her tone was tart. She was shocked to hear him laugh quietly. So he had some emotions after all.

"You know," she said, "it would be nice if we talked about something. Like who you are."

He was slow to respond. "I am *not* an open book. A nerd friend of mine has removed me from every possible database. I have to be private to do this job."

She hadn't even thought about that. Pondering for a few minutes, she then asked, "Can you erase *me*?"

"Not if you ever want a piece of your life back. I doubt you'd want to be nobody."

He had a point.

A couple of minutes later he spoke again. "I promised you could call your friends. One friend. She can let the others know you're alive. But it has to be a circumspect conversation. I'll tell you how."

Of course he would. Even directing her conversations with friends now. But given all he was doing to make them untraceable, she understood. Hated it but understood.

Eventually the storm clouds lightened enough to reveal low-hanging cumulus. Lightning expressed the rage of the heavens ever more frequently. Then a drowning downpour began, locking them into an even smaller cocoon. Silvery drizzles of rain poured everywhere until Hale turned on front and back wipers.

Even those weren't much help.

"Hale?"

"Yeah?"

"Do you have any idea where we're going? An end point?"

Once again that delay before he answered. "I'm doing my best to prevent you from going to hell."

The calm way he spoke was as scary as his words.

Allie subsided into her seat, watching the storm darken the growing day.

MIDMORNING BROUGHT ANOTHER roadside diner. Allie sighed. "I think I'm going to have the measure of every grill man between home and the Rockies."

"You could know a worse bunch of people."

Which she apparently already did.

She waited in the car without being told to as Hale filled the gas tank. Then, once again, they did the unexpected and drove away without sampling the diner's menu.

He probably thought he was reassuring her as he said, "I believe there's another small town ahead. We'll find a place there for lunch."

"Do you carry a detailed map in your head?"

"It helps if I open one every night."

"I never saw you do that."

"Not everything I do has to be visible."

Far from it, Allie thought. Inscrutable and now invisible. Or maybe the other way around, since he'd erased himself from every database.

She tried to imagine what it would be like to erase her entire past, to walk forward in life with all those years consigned to a void.

"Do you ever want to be a normal guy?" she asked.

"I never have been. But what's normal anyway? Only what someone else thinks it is."

She turned that around in her mind as more miles slipped away. Hale might be right. How did she make herself feel normal? By fitting in with a group, by feeling she belonged and was like them. Was that everyone's normal?

Her "lunch bunch," as she and her friends liked to call themselves. A group of women diverse in their backgrounds but most working for Ellis. Some they had known since college. A band of women on similar wavelengths with similar interests. But that's what helped build bonds, wasn't it?

They reached a small town that looked hospitable despite a sky that promised vengeance.

"There's a café here," Hale said. "You might be able to get a meal more to your liking."

He pulled a U-turn around a median that had clearly been constructed to enhance the town's appearance. It left barely enough room on either side to allow parallel parking. He wheeled into a space with the ease of a pro. Allie couldn't remember the last time she had done that. Diagonal parking was the best.

"There it is," he said, pointing.

The rain had lightened to a sprinkle. Allie climbed out of the car feeling every cramped and stiffened muscle from all the time spent driving. She wondered if the kinks might become permanent.

She also felt awkward in her new clothes. Like a misfit. She must present a dumpy picture, unlike her usually smartly dressed self.

But then she realized from glancing at people around her that she didn't look out of place. Not here. The town seemed to be populated by folks who worked at physically demanding jobs, the kinds of jobs that kept them in old clothes. Perhaps kept them unable to afford anything fancier.

Inside, the café was decorated in red gingham curtains and matching tablecloths beneath plastic protectors. The vinyl seats echoed the red. The menu picked up on the theme.

A pleasingly plump young waitress brought them menus with a smile and asked if they wanted coffee.

"A gallon might do for me," Hale answered, looking at Allie. "You?"

"Coffee will be fine."

An insulated carafe accompanied by blue ceramic mugs along with a saucer of small cups of half-and-half. Allie didn't take much time to scan the menu. A turkey club sandwich? With actual lettuce and tomato? Heaven. Plus her side of salad so she could feel like she wasn't persistently poisoning herself.

For the first time it occurred to her that she might need some adjustments to her thinking. About food in particular. Only now did she realize that she had grown picky. Maybe even snobbish about food and clothes. The idea didn't make her feel any better about herself.

"I was lucky in my childhood," she offered. She didn't want silence, especially while sharing a meal.

Hale picked up the baton and ran with it. "How so?"

"My dad was a cop, a close friend of Max's. Mom taught elementary school. They loved me and I never doubted it. Not many people can say that from what I've seen."

"No, they can't." He revealed nothing by tone or expression.

"My life crashed down around me the day my dad stopped to help a motorist with a broken-down car. A pickup never saw them, and to this day I can't imagine why flashing lights didn't catch his attention. Anyway, the pickup hit the back of Dad's vehicle with my dad right in the middle between the patrol car and the disabled car."

"God."

"*She* had nothing to do with it," she replied, echoing Max. "But my dad, do you know what his last act was? To shove the driver of the disabled vehicle to the side of the road just before the truck hit. With his last breath, my dad saved a man's life."

"Remarkable man."

"I think so. I've always tried to live up to him but I'm pretty sure I haven't succeeded."

She stared at the remains of her sandwich, her appetite lost. Why had she brought that up at this time?

Then she looked out the window at people passing

on the street and she knew. They were the people her dad would have identified with. Not with the woman she'd become.

"Can I take this with me?" she asked.

"Sure. And more if you want." Hale was eating a double portion of fries and a juicy-looking roast beef sandwich. "It may be a while before we stop again."

She expelled a slow breath between her lips. "Of course it will. How was your childhood?"

"I didn't have one." End of subject.

Did he mean that for real or was that just his answer to protect his secrecy? But something about him suddenly struck to her core. It was the truth. Whatever lay in his past, especially his childhood, was better forgotten. It must have been dreadful.

THEIR NEXT STOP came at dusk in a busy truck stop. Multiple large eighteen-wheelers grumbled in side-by-side slots. The sun hadn't appeared all day, and now the air felt pregnant with ozone.

Hale handed her one of his phones. "Keep it short. Don't give them a hint of where you are or what you're doing."

She spoke drily. "Basically tell them that I'm alive and not to worry."

"No more than that. One call, so pick wisely. Like I said, you don't want to pull them into this mess."

No, she didn't. She imagined goons trying to get her location out of her friends, and the image wasn't pretty. "It's not as if I know where I am."

The problem was, she discovered, that because of

the convenience of modern phones, she hadn't memorized phone numbers. "Ah, crap," she muttered, and ransacked her brain. At last Shawna's number emerged from the scramble, and she tried it.

She was relieved to get Shawna's voice mail, which exonerated her from explaining anything. "Shawna, I just want to let you know I'm alive and I'm fine. Tell you all about it later." She hoped. Then she let go of the brief link to her friend and watched Hale shove it into the back of a truck. Some poor driver was going to carry the thing for hundreds of miles now.

Hale made a call from yet another burner. He kept his voice too low for her to hear much over the growling engines all around her.

When at last he disconnected and pulled the battery and SIM out, he looked at her. "Ellis has definitely put his security team on finding you. Let's eat, then get the hell out of Dodge."

"For real?" Ellis's security team really was looking for her? A rivulet of ice dribbled down her neck. She couldn't help darting her gaze around as if some horror was about to emerge from the deepening shadows around these trucks.

If Ellis was using his security apparatus to find her, then there was no question of what was going on. Her last, small doubt washed away.

But before they departed, Hale got down on the ground and ran a piece of equipment beneath the vehicle. Ten minutes later, he emerged with a small black box. He tossed it in the nearby trash bin.

"What was that?"

"A transmitter. Time to ditch it."

"You knew it was there?"

He shook his head, but she couldn't tell if that was a negative.

ALLIE WAS GROWING used to the rhythm of her new life. Food twice a day whenever Hale felt they could stop. She had to eat or get carryout to avoid hunger.

The truck-stop diner was busy, full of boisterous men who seemed glad of company and glad to be out of their truck cabs. She envied them.

The menu offered a cornucopia of hearty foods. Allie shut down the last of her guilt and helped herself without regard to all the dietary habits she'd learned. It was, she admitted, more like the cooking she'd grown up with.

Pea soup, always her favorite. A ham and Swiss on a crusty roll. Even a piece of pie. Well, she could spend hours in the gym whenever this flight was over. Then she squashed such thoughts and decided to be glad that she could fill her stomach and ease her hunger. She even felt okay about walking out with a paper bag holding a few pastries. Nights could be long.

They didn't dawdle. Hale gave her the chance to stretch her legs for maybe ten minutes, and he seemed as glad to move around himself.

Then it was off into the deepening night with a sleazy motel somewhere ahead.

"They can't have followed me this fast," Allie said. Was she trying to reassure herself?

"You're making a mistake," Hale answered.

"How?"

"You're forgetting that Ellis's team can reach out almost anywhere in the world. That's why we're not stopping. That's why we won't stop until I can get a bead on the threat and hopefully shrink it."

Maybe the most unnerving thing was that she was beginning to believe in this crazy world she'd fallen into.

Her life no longer sounded like a bad movie script. It had *become* one.

HALE SENSED THE shift in Allie's reaction to the threat marching toward her. It hadn't been easy for her.

But why should it have been? She'd apparently grown up in a happy family with a father who went out to round up bad guys every day and probably never spoke of what he saw or had to do. Her mother had likely come home from teaching with a cute or charming story many days. Even her father's death had been an accident, not murder.

How could Allie have known about the evil beneath her bright world? How could she have suspected there were shadows in which *real* monsters lurked?

Her innocence was shattering right before his eyes and he had to let the destruction continue in order to protect her. Most of his clients had possessed a more realistic view of the dangers, but not Allie. She evidently had been protected her entire life.

He could have hated himself right then but resisted the urge. He had to allow this. It was part of his job.

It was part of keeping Allie safe. But it was still ugly to behold.

Hale had learned from his earliest days that life could be painful, hideous, even horrific. In the end, he had come to believe that he could trust only himself.

Maybe that was why he had joined the military, where faith in your unit was demanded, where you had to have your comrade's back. Or maybe the biggest reason was to grow strong, to face fear, to never doubt his abilities again.

But war had changed his entire direction. He'd made up his mind to spend his life helping people. His first attempt, by joining a security company, had crashed and burned. So he had started his own *personal* protection business. Taking care of individuals instead of being hired out as a mercenary.

Now he was racing across the countryside with a woman who didn't deserve to be tangled in this hell.

At least his men had been able to plant tracers on most of Ellis's men, providing him with more information so he could help Allie better.

He might even be helping strangers, in the case of Ellis. A perk.

It would sure make Max's life better. He doubted that Allie had any idea that Max had been heading up the investigation of Ellis for years now except for the brief bit he'd told her. Max would probably dance on air with his mastiff if he could get Ellis.

Hale decided to break the silence even if it went against his grain. To distract Allie. "That dog of Max's is something else."

He sensed Allie stir beside him.

"Yeah," she answered. "I sometimes think Harvey is at least twice his size."

"And obedient only when he chooses to be. Damn smart dog."

"Smart how?"

"He's in charge."

That pulled a small laugh from her. "I think Max knows it."

"He doesn't care. He dotes on that pooch."

When Allie didn't reply, he thought he'd reached a conversational dead end. He was good at that. He tried again.

"I bet you didn't know that mastiffs were used as draft animals in the First World War."

Another laugh escaped her. "Come on."

"I'm being serious. They pulled munitions carts. I wonder about that."

"Using dogs that way?"

"Nah," he replied. "Using mastiffs. They're famous for sitting down and refusing to budge when they feel tired. Read about one guy who swore he takes a wheelbarrow with him on long walks with his dog in case the animal decides he's had enough."

"Oh, Lord. I've never seen Harvey do that."

"Probably because Max learned that lesson long ago. Maybe they take short enough walks together."

"Well, Harvey is stubborn. I can easily see him just plopping his butt down."

"I enjoy watching the two of them together. Max *really* dotes."

"Dogs are easy to dote on." There was a smile in her voice.

"You have one?"

"Not since high school."

And that seemed to be the end of conversation. Again. Well, he'd kept that running longer than he usually did. Not that he cared. Shooting the breeze had never appealed to him.

But he sharply felt Allie's need for more than staring out a car window. Well, he got it. He'd rather be doing something else, too. He'd have preferred to hike this trip.

Unfortunately, he could think of nothing more to talk about.

Fifty miles later, it was Allie who spoke. "Why do you do this, Hale?"

"Someone has to."

"But people can hire all kinds of security around their homes and so on."

"That might be enough for some. It's not good enough for some."

"Why not?"

"Sometimes it's best to trust only one person. Less chance for loose lips and bribery."

"I didn't think of that," she admitted. "But this must be as boring for you as it is for me."

"Not quite. I have to stay on high alert."

"Watching everything. I kind of noticed. But that still doesn't explain *why*."

He sighed inwardly, then gave the short answer. Maybe the only one he had. "Because people need protection."

"You're helping people."

He didn't respond to that. He didn't see himself as a caped crusader of any kind. He didn't think he was on a mission of mercy. He just had a set of skills that were useful for protecting people. It was something, anyway.

"You said you were going to get a bead on these people. How?"

He didn't answer her question but diverted. "We'll have a face-to-face when I find one or two. My contacts are working on it."

"Then?"

"I'm going to do some serious interrogation."

ALLIE DIDN'T ASK for details. Ugly images from movies and TV sprang to her mind and she hoped he didn't mean *that* kind of interrogation.

Probably not, she decided. While she had felt the granite within him, she'd also noticed that so far he was a decent man. More decent than many of the men she worked with who seemed to be incapable of talking to her face. But stripping her with their eyes? Some kind of male failing?

But not with this man.

Satisfied, at least as much as she could be, she resettled herself in her seat and dozed. One way of making this endless travel easier.

As she drifted away, she remembered the comic books her parents had bought for her when they faced a long car drive. She wondered if those characters were still around.

IT MAY HAVE been hours later. Allie had no idea because she'd slept a bit, but Hale at last pulled into another motel. It looked about as appetizing as the previous ones.

A bedroom, a bathroom. This one with double beds and coverlets as outdated as the rest of the place. She stifled a sigh and let him carry in whatever he chose. Life had slipped from her hands into his. For the moment, she'd let it be.

"In the morning," he remarked, "I'll get us some more clothes. You especially."

"But that's wasteful. We have clothes."

"We're not going to stop at a coin laundry to spend two hours."

Well, that made sense. She sat on the edge of the bed, watching him drop two duffels. His and hers. They ought to be labeled, like towels.

"Then I'm going to need more underwear," she informed him. "I guess you can say your wife is sick."

All he replied was to ask her what sizes. And there went the last of her lacy garments. Oh, well.

He showered first since she insisted. That was something *she* could control and she had begun to feel mulish again. Maybe she wouldn't shower at all. A day skipped would hardly make her smell bad.

While he occupied the bathroom, she changed into that flannel nightgown. It proved to be soft and warm and she decided she liked it. Then she crawled into bed beneath the questionable coverlet onto sheets that felt and smelled clean. A plus.

Her mistake was in not turning her back to the bathroom door. When Hale emerged, he wore only a towel around his narrow hips. With the only light coming from the bathroom behind him, she could see only his general outline and a bit of his muscling across his chest and in his arms.

She snapped her eyes closed immediately. Too much. Too good. Honed muscles, not for show, and likely a washboard belly. Boy, she had friends who agonized in gyms trying to get those abs. But they seemed of a piece with the rest of the man.

Yeah, she wished she could open her eyes again and just stare, but Hale didn't invite that. He was a focused man, trained for action, certainly not for riding around in a car day and night.

Rustling suggested he pulled on some pants. Then she heard his breathing speed up a bit, and she at last opened her eyes.

He was on the floor at the foot of the bed doing pushups. Then deep knee bends, then thrusts, then sit-ups, then some other exercises she couldn't name.

Heck, she ought to do that, too. Before she calcified in the shape of a car seat. But not now. Not in her nightgown.

Just about the time she heard him slide into the next bed, she drifted off. She hadn't had nightmares in many years, but she had them that night.

THEY CHECKED OUT of the motel well before dawn. Allie's sleep had been restless and she didn't hesitate to yawn openly, however impolite. The silvery moon from the start of their trip had vanished. New moon, she decided, although she rarely paid attention to the moon.

This was a lousy time of year to travel, she thought. Winter was blowing in everywhere. They had begun to see patches of snow, and the air was turning colder. This morning she could see her breath.

"What's on the menu today?" she asked irritably.

"Some beautiful mountains. Enjoy them."

That sounded more like an order than a suggestion. She snapped on her seat belt. What was the choice? She needed to find one soon, before she erupted like Vesuvius.

They had their usual truck-stop breakfast, no better or worse than those that had come before. It was still dark when they began rolling again.

The ground rose steadily, then she saw the first flakes of snow. "Couldn't you have taken us by a southern route?"

"More people."

Well, that answered her. Maybe. "If this snow gets heavier, it's going to be hard to drive." Especially for a Southern California girl who'd seen it only in the Sierras. She'd never had to drive in it, though.

"I've done it before."

She supposed that was meant to be reassuring. It wasn't. Very little about this trek was reassuring.

As the snow thickened, the roads remained clear for a while. Their climb continued. Then she saw a sign that at last told her where she was:

Nez Perce Reservation.

"We're in Idaho!"

"So it would appear."

She thought over the days of travel, which at the rate they were going probably should have carried them most of the way to the East Coast. It also gave her a good idea how winding a route Hale had chosen. Avoiding large towns, sticking to out-of-the-way places...

It was a wonder her head hadn't spun. They must have backtracked on different roads more than once.

She would have loved to know how he planned this. Evasion. It was incredible.

She spoke again. "You heard anything from your contacts?" He'd called again last night.

"Yes. Ellis's security seems to have concluded that we headed north."

"How could they have done that?"

"My guys are checking on that. They're keeping an eye out."

His guys. She wondered who made up this invisible web of contacts. How many there were. Did he employ them or just rely on friends? He wouldn't be likely to tell her.

"We'll change our general direction soon," Hale announced.

"Well, that might be warmer."

The falling snow thickened. It began to stick to the pavement. Then at some road or another, he took a right turn, presumably moving them southward. More tiny towns spaced far apart.

At long last, he parked in front of a store, an aging structure that fit the town around it. *Dilapidated* would have been a kind term.

"Clothes," he said. He tossed her a faded green hat that was crushed and wrinkled. It looked like something a fisherman might wear. "Wear that, don't take it off, and keep your head down."

She put it on, wondering why she needed it.

He astonished her. "You're coming in. Just don't choose something that will stand out because I'll take it from your hands."

That sounded like a threat. After all this, however, she was willing to accept his dictum. Standing out would not be a good thing.

Inside, the store was quiet. Hardly another customer. The plump sales lady jumped to help them. A grandmotherly looking woman, she might have owned the store.

"Stocking up for a long hike," Hale said in answer to the woman's question.

"In this weather?" The clerk pretended a shiver. "You're braver than I am."

Hale managed a rusty smile. "Not as bad as jumping naked into a hole in the ice."

The woman laughed, then left them alone to pick out their items.

Inwardly sighing, Allie followed directions. A pair of dully colored flannel shirts, distinguished only by the fact that they tried to appear plaid. More jeans. Socks. And the underwear, plain white briefs.

No taste in this town, she thought. Or maybe taste was unaffordable.

"You come to join the militia?" the clerk asked as she checked them out.

"Could be," was Hale's inscrutable answer.

The woman smiled. "Then you'll be back for camo, unless you want to get it now. We've got plenty in the back."

"We'll wait and see if we're welcome."

"Might be a good idea." She waved them on their way.

At the car, Hale put their bags in the back. Once inside, as they drove away again, Allie could no longer contain herself.

"Militia?"

"Idaho collects a lot of survivalists, mostly up north. And some get together in bands."

"Oh, man."

"You must have read about it."

"It seems they don't make the headlines."

"They don't want to."

Another glimpse of a new world, Allie thought. She'd had a general idea that militias existed but she hadn't much thought about where. Here, apparently.

"It was a good cover," Hale said.

Allie turned her head toward him. "You expected that?"

"Not necessarily that we'd be asked, but I was sure that would be the interpretation."

He was always thinking ahead and living in a world Allie had never met. It seemed Hale could navigate almost anything, and she felt her first glimmer of reluctant respect.

THAT NIGHT, AFTER the usual roadside dinner, they stopped at yet another awful motel. How did Hale find these places?

But this constant running and driving was exhausting her.

"Can't we at least spend an extra night somewhere?" Although what she'd do with the time… Oh, heck. Just avoiding more road miles would have been great.

"No."

If she could have, she might well have shaken him. "I'm paying for your services," she said point-blank. "I ought to have something to say about this!"

"I'm doing what you're paying me to do. You don't have to like it."

Well, that was the end of that argument. If it had indeed been an argument.

He emptied the duffel of all her previous clothes and put the new ones in it. At least he didn't switch out the flannel nightgown. *Something* remained.

"They surely can't find us overnight," she remarked, another stab at disagreement.

He straightened from his own duffel and faced her. "Someone could. It only takes one."

"Sheesh." She shut up. She had a feeling that if she simply refused to get into his car, he wouldn't leave her standing in the middle of nowhere. No, he'd probably pick her up bodily and place her in the seat.

She glowered at him as she sat on the edge of the bed. Tonight there was only one bed, a double. He'd be sleeping on the floor again.

Hale gave her plenty of privacy, but no solitude, a distinction she was learning. It was also one she didn't like.

"How are you going to know when we're safe?" she asked a while later.

"I will."

"Your invisible contacts, I presume."

"No. I'll catch whoever. I'm good at that."

"Is there anything you're not good at?"

"Talking."

She rolled her eyes, then grabbed her nightwear and headed to the bathroom. She wished she'd purchased shower shoes. Blech.

"I'm going to step outside and make another call."

Of course he was. The calls seemed to be coming closer together. Had he learned something that worried him?

She'd never know, she guessed. But maybe that ought to worry *her*.

Oh, hell. What was the point? For once in her life, she had absolutely no control.

OUTSIDE, IN A night so quiet Hale could hear his own breaths, he placed a call to a memorized number.

"Are we having vegetable stew?" he asked.

"Hearty and it makes you hale. A great meal." Stu paused. Then, "I can scarcely believe it, but the host has hired a professional chef."

Hale tensed until his teeth clenched in a rictus. He didn't need an interpreter. *Chef* meant *assassin*. While his eyes never stopped scanning the immediate area, his mind began to spin around possibilities. "Okay."

"Does she have the recipe?" Did Allie possess any written or recorded information?

"Only in her memory. Maybe she should have written it down."

"No use now."

"When is the chef supposed to arrive?"

"No idea. I'm going to check on that. To get the kitchen ready. I hear a few of the sous chefs are on their way."

"Already?" Several security men were on their way, too. Hale paused, then decided to take the risk again. "Why. I'd a thought it would be too soon."

"Ya think?" Stu replied. "I'll check. Maybe I can find the damn chef."

Hale disconnected, yanked the battery from the phone and put the burner on a car with Oregon plates.

An assassin was on the way? Why weren't the security people enough? And how were he and Allie being tracked? Stu had understood the code last night, and now he knew that Hale and Allie were somewhere between Idaho and Wyoming. Because how else could Stu and the others hope to find out how close the threat had come? Or maybe to locate the threat themselves?

Hale had needed to reveal that they were at the border between Wyoming and Idaho only because of the "chef," but he'd chosen his words judiciously. *Why. I'd a.* No one overhearing should have grasped that as a location reference.

He stood outside for a long time, rocking on his heels. This had gone way over the top. Way, way over. Why would Ellis bring a professional killer into this?

Because Allie knew something extremely dangerous, and it didn't matter if it was on paper or a computer flash drive. She had to be permanently silenced. Completely silenced.

Hale swore quietly. It wasn't as if he couldn't deal with a pro. He knew their methods and their mindsets very well. But this tracking thing…

Why were the security guards even out there, given the assassin? Did they know a pro was looking, as well? Or did they have some inside information they were following, possibly unaware that the pro was tracking *them*?

Inside information. Hale's gut twisted. Had one of his team sold out? Or talked too loosely?

All of a sudden staying here seemed like too much of a risk. Stu knew they were somewhere along the border, but he didn't know which direction they'd take. They had to skedaddle *now*.

But he sure as hell wasn't going to tell Allie about the pro. She didn't need any more worries.

At last he went inside. In the dim light from the bathroom, he saw Allie in bed with the covers drawn up to her chin. He also saw that her eyes were wide-open.

"Get up," he said. "We're leaving now."

"Why? It's too soon."

"Just do it."

"I deserve an explanation!"

"If a gator was nipping at your heels would you argue with me or just jump away?"

She gasped, then threw the covers back. "But you're going to tell me when we get on the road. I've had enough of being kept in the dark!"

He didn't bother to argue. He'd already gathered the clothes they needed to trash into the shopping bags. For just an instant he considered leaving them behind.

No. Now was not a good time to change his habits. Leave no trail.

Except somehow the breadcrumbs were out there. He'd probably spend the next few days racking his brain trying to figure out how he'd gone wrong. Or *who* had gone wrong.

Chapter Five

Once they were on the road again, Allie didn't press him for an explanation. Instead she fell asleep in the seat beside him.

Which left him entirely too much time to ramble inside his own head. For the first time he considered that silence was not always the best way to handle life.

But considering how many times as a child he'd been swatted or mistreated for opening his mouth, silence had become his friend.

Not this night. He'd have cheerfully gabbed about some of the bars he'd visited or questioned her about her life before Ellis.

Anything but feeling the knife of betrayal turning in his gut. What the hell had gone wrong? Stu would suspect it, too. He'd start guarding information, start looking for one of the guys who was acting unusually.

In the meantime, he had to lower their profile even more. Maybe not give Stu another hint of the course they were taking.

If he'd been inclined to such displays, he might have hammered his fist on the steering wheel.

Before dawn, he saw an unattended dumpster near the road. He pulled over, left the engine running so Allie wouldn't get cold, and pulled the bags out of the back. He emptied them into the bin but kept the bags. Next stop to fling them. No trail, no trace.

Then they took off again. And, of course, Allie woke up.

"Where are we?" she asked drowsily.

"Between here and there, in the middle of nowhere." Or so he had thought. He tweaked the heater to blow more warm air on her. She needed a blanket, he decided. Maybe a neck pillow.

Hell, someone might know *he* was a part of this flight. Yeah, he'd switched license plates in the dead of night while Allie slept, but maybe that hadn't been enough. Maybe putting his plates on a different car had caught the owner's eye and it had been reported.

But so fast? Most people looked at their plates only when they put a new sticker on them.

Or maybe that person had been ticketed.

He smothered a sigh, the hamster wheel of his thoughts driving him nuts. Then came the question from Allie.

"Why did we have to leave so quickly?"

"Because I seem to have left some breadcrumbs behind."

He felt her sit up straighter. "I don't see how that's possible!"

"I'm trying to work it out so it doesn't happen again."

Clearly she wasn't reassured. "Good God, Hale, you've been driving us everywhere but straight. Nobody's got anything they could track. I don't believe this."

It wasn't a choice. He didn't *want* to believe it. He *had* to.

Time passed, then Allie spoke again. "Could there be a transmitter on this car?"

"I swept the thing. I got rid of it."

How it had gotten there was still a mystery. He had left the car in her parking garage while he made her pack up. Could she have already been under such close watch? It didn't seem likely but it wasn't impossible. He wanted to hammer his fist on the wheel again. She'd gone to work that day. She'd left Max's almost immediately with him. The getaway had been too fast to have been anything but clean.

Hell's bells. There was only one thing left to do. "Next time I see an option, I may buy a new vehicle."

"But that'll involve all kinds of paperwork!"

"Not a street sale. It won't be easy to find a baby this good, though."

"No, it won't. Plus it'll have all kinds of equipment you'll need to yank out."

"Done it before."

She subsided, twisting until she stared out the side window at the ink of the night speeding past them.

The ice between them came from more than the weather outside.

ALLIE CLOSED HER eyes but she wasn't sleeping as the first rosy light of dawn appeared on the passenger side of the car. Heading north again?

Maybe it would have been better to face out this threat in LA. It would at least have been more comfortable.

On the other hand, she didn't think Hale was doing this because it was fun. He had honestly believed he needed to take her away. Now he must be feeling just awful. Or worse, stupid.

But stupid was the last thing she would have accused him of. There were plenty of other epithets she could have applied, but she no longer felt like it.

Now she decided they were *both* in trouble. If these bad guys found her, would they stop with her? Maybe they'd go after Hale, too. She felt ashamed that she hadn't thought earlier that he might be risking his neck, too.

The sky was no longer leaden. A bright day began to be born. As long as they didn't turn the wrong direction right into bad weather, anyway. She could see pregnant clouds over the mountains to her side. Which mountains?

She hardly cared. Alligators nipping at her heels. They must be close for him to have pulled her out of bed before she'd even slept.

"Can you drive faster?" she asked him.

That drew a rare laugh from him. "Sure, so I can spend some time talking to a cop about a speeding ticket. Nailed."

Another thing she hadn't considered. "But you have fake IDs."

"Sure. And stolen plates on the car."

She blinked. "My God."

"Now you know."

She chewed her lip, then had an idea. "What about getting me a fake ID?"

"No."

"No?"

"Lady, I may break some laws, but I'm not going to allow you to. If we ever get you back to a normal life, it's going to be your own. And you're not going to live in fear that someone will catch you out on your ID. That's jail time."

She swallowed hard. This swamp just kept getting deeper. Only remembering Max telling her how other Ellis employees had died or disappeared kept her from calling this whole thing off.

What could Ellis do to her? A lot, evidently.

Glumly, she watched the breaking day, unable to enjoy the beauty of it.

"A new car? Really?"

"Maybe not." As usual he said no more.

HALE FELT LIKE a stinking pile of manure. There was something he hadn't considered, not the least of them a mole in his crew. But a transmitter? He supposed he could figure that one out quickly enough, and without replacing his car.

A detector for RF frequencies occupied a compartment in his trunk. He should have used it again sooner. Well, he'd use it before this day was over. Definitely. Put his mind at rest about one thing.

He was getting as restless as Allie. This perpetual

running went against his grain. He preferred action, preferred facing threats head-on.

But this was different. The people he'd protected in the past had limited enemies. Maybe a drug gang. Maybe just one person.

Ellis was a whole different kettle of fish. He exceeded the threat any gang could present. Tentacles everywhere. Eyes everywhere. And methods of keeping any blame far away from him.

He doubted a drug cartel could pose as many dangers. Ellis operated right in the open as a respected businessman. His was no cover story. It was a *clean* story.

Until they could nail him with something. That was the thing. He had to help Max crucify this guy or Allie could never sleep easily again.

But right then, he was learning nothing about the enemy. Instead he was running. He hated this.

"Allie?"

"Yes?"

"Did you take any paper, files or computer flash drives from your office?"

"Good God, no! That would have been stealing. Violation of protected company secrets."

He nodded into the dawning day. "So you have no proof."

"No…" Her voice sounded thin. "None."

"I bet your memory is pretty good, though."

"Well, yes, but I can't prove anything. That's why I can't understand this. I have *nothing*."

"How's Ellis supposed to be sure of that? And Ellis would know about your relationship with Max."

Allie stirred in her seat restlessly. "Hale? I didn't drag Max into this mess, did I?" Then before he could respond, she murmured, "Oh, Max, what have I done?"

Hale's hands clenched on the steering wheel until his knuckles must have turned white. Beneath his leather gloves, they were hidden.

"Allie."

"What?" she answered gloomily.

"You didn't do a damn thing wrong. You're an accountant. You found an error in the company books. You took it to the boss, who said he'd handle it. *He* was the one who made the veiled threat against you."

"But Max…"

"Trust me, Max knew exactly what he was stepping into. He knows all about Ellis. But what were you supposed to do? Cut off a guy you've known your entire life? Pretend he'd vanished when you didn't even know that you'd been threatened?"

"I guess." Her tone hadn't improved.

"Believe me, not understanding that you'd been threatened, why in the world should you avoid Max?"

"I don't know. Maybe I shouldn't have told him my little story, which I thought was amusing at the time."

Hale relaxed his grip on the steering wheel. "Ellis won't go after Max."

She drew a quick breath. "How can you be sure of that?"

"Because Max is a cop. Max has been investigating Ellis for years. If something happens to him, the rest of the team are going to point their eyes right at Ellis. Worse scrutiny than now. Max should be safe."

He hoped that had helped, but he wasn't sure. It had

been pretty thin, his yarn about Max being safe. Allie was no fool. He just hoped she didn't think this one through.

He needed to do more for this woman, to fill her days with something besides endless driving and scenery, which, while it could be beautiful, palled after so long.

But the noose was drawing tighter, and he couldn't afford to slow them down, not yet. Maybe never, at least until he had a real idea how to protect her.

"You ever been married?" he heard himself ask. Where the hell had that come from? He didn't usually ask personal questions.

"No. Not even close."

That surprised him a bit. "Why not close? A woman as pretty as you…"

"That's exactly the problem," she said tartly. "Some guy will have to realize that I'm more than a pair of boobs walking around on top of his version of heaven."

It was a good thing that he didn't have anything in his mouth just then. It would have sprayed all over the windshield.

"Wow," was all that escaped him.

"Well, it's true," she said sourly. "They think I'm an idiot. I'm not. Having sex if I want it would be easy. I don't need any entanglements unless there's real respect."

"You go," he said approvingly. "But I've never met anyone who had your way with a turn of phrase."

"Maybe just not a woman who's so blunt."

That was possible. He'd never lived in a woman's

world so he had no idea what had made Allie feel this way. He applauded her opinion nonetheless.

"I gather you decided this from experience?"

"Since I was fifteen or so. Nothing has changed it."

"I guess you met a lot of boors."

"That's a kind description."

Maybe it was. How much did women put up with that he'd never noticed? Probably a lot.

"Men need to corral their eyes and their hands," she added. "But it goes beyond that. I always pay my own way on a date. I learned not to let a guy buy me dinner because then he thinks I owe him something."

"Well, damn," he said. "Just *damn*."

"Where have you been living, Hale?"

"On a different planet."

A tiny laugh escaped her. "I could have guessed that."

A rare smile cracked his face.

NEARING MIDDAY, ANOTHER truck stop appeared. Apparently, the country's lifeblood sometimes traveled along roads other than major arteries. Not all of them were big rigs, however. A number of them, large as they were, appeared to be smaller shipments.

Hale pulled something out of a compartment in the back of the car and Allie watched him walk around the vehicle, bending down and occasionally getting on his knees. He looked like a man who'd heard an unusual sound from his undercarriage. Then he lifted the hood.

A man wearing a heavily lined denim jacket walked

over to them, pulling his pants up over a sagging belly. "Need some help, friend?"

"I think I got it," Hale said, reaching into the engine. "Been over some rough roads. Thought I might be slipping a tire belt, but not that I can see. This damn alternator cap, though. Sometimes it just goes loose on me, so I tighten it up."

"You might want to use some wire over those tabs," the guy said, and strode away.

"Good idea," Hale called after him. "Thanks."

He slammed the hood shut, then put his equipment in the rear. "Let's go," he said to Allie.

"No lunch?"

"Not here. We just got noticed."

She'd given up sighing and, for now, arguing. He'd presented her too much food for thought that morning, and she was still digesting it.

Once they were on the road, he said, "No transmitter that I could detect."

"Then what could it be?"

Hale didn't answer.

Before long, however, he spied an aging pickup standing alone on a small dirt turnout and pulled up behind it. Allie couldn't see a soul in sight.

"Close your eyes," he said. "Theft is about to occur."

But she couldn't close her eyes. He went to the trunk, then came around front. With what looked like a wrench in his hand, he lifted the hood once again.

No other vehicles passed them. A quiet road in the early afternoon.

Three minutes later, he closed the hood, returned to

the rear and threw something inside with a clatter. A minute after that, they were driving again.

"What did you do?"

"If you must know, I just heisted that man's plates. I didn't leave mine behind. In a few more hours I'll do it again. Don't ask any more, Allie. You don't want to be complicit."

"Like I could tell anyone. I doubt it's a major crime anyway."

"Major or minor, you don't need a record."

Their next stop was a drive-through on the edge of another small town. At least this one boasted a grilled chicken sandwich, which appealed to her a lot more than a burger of dubious lineage. Hale tripled her order and added a large soda. He ordered plenty for himself.

They didn't even stop to eat.

"You're driving like someone is right behind us," she remarked, fear causing her heart to skip.

"Not that close. No way. But I don't want to give them a chance."

Then some tired Christmas decorations began to show up on the widely spread houses. Ranches? She had no idea as they turned up into the mountains again. The decorations disappeared.

They pulled in for the night at a small lodge that looked downscale. Probably for cheap skiers, but there wasn't enough snow nearby to draw them.

"Just let me sleep tonight," she told Hale. "Damn it, I need some time when I'm not crunched up like a pretzel. I'd stay two nights but…"

"But I won't let you. Not now."

"Or ever," she muttered, pulling out her nightgown.

HALE WENT OUTSIDE. He'd really screwed up somewhere. Now he wondered if he should even call Stu again. Too soon. If he did, however, he wasn't going to give Stu a clue as to where they were. Not this time. Maybe not for a while.

Once again, he ran his meter under and around the car. Then he found it. Small. Intermittent bursts. Easy to miss.

He yanked it out, then checked for a duplicate. When he was satisfied, he threw the transmitter into the metal box with his phones. The box was a Faraday cage and would allow no electronic transmissions in or out. Maybe he'd need the transmitter later.

In fact, the only good news was that he didn't have a traitor working against them.

Then he went in to tell Allie they were hitting the road again. Because, sure, he just loved to tell her that.

This time she turned into a hornet's nest. "This has got to stop, Hale! I get that you're protecting me, but I can't go on like this indefinitely. I'd be surprised if you can, either."

"I sure as hell don't want to."

"Then find a way we can stop for a little while. Get out of that damned car. Just to take a long walk. Hike up a mountain, build a snowman. *Anything!*"

"It would be too dangerous to stop now. They followed us to this point."

She clenched her jaw. "Some bodyguard you are. Get out so I can dress."

He'd deserved that. Absolutely deserved it. There'd been a hole in his assessment of the situation before they left LA, a great big gaping hole.

He kicked his own butt harder than she ever could.

The only thing that struck him was that, given he'd been carrying a transmitter, the bad guys were too far behind. It was taking them too long.

Why?

Endless night miles fell behind them as he beat his brain to understand exactly what was happening here.

ALLIE WAS ANGRIER than she'd ever been in her life. They'd been driving hither and yon all over the place, stealing license plates, and carrying a *transmitter*?

How the hell had he missed it when he checked earlier? Him and his fancy equipment, his burner phones and a car stripped of everything that might emit a signal. How the hell?

If she hadn't sensed the anger in him, she'd have erupted again. He was mad at himself. Oh, poor baby.

She snorted and tried to wrap her jacket more closely around herself. At night she usually felt a little cold, but this was worse. A frigid night combined with lack of sleep. She wondered if she would ever feel warm again.

Without a word, Hale reached over and turned up the heater.

She didn't bother to thank him.

Hours passed before he spoke again. "I was thinking that perhaps that transmitter was placed before we left LA."

"When?" she asked acidly. "Why would they put it on your car instead of mine?"

"Maybe when I came to your apartment with you. I thought it was too soon for them to be worried. You'd been to work that day after all. No reason to expect you wouldn't return the next day."

"You said that. Well, you're right about that, although apparently not, given what you found. Hell, I came home from work, went over to Max's for an early dinner…" Her voice trailed off.

"Max," she said. "I went to see Max. A detective. Then you came."

"Maybe." How would anyone know why he'd gone there? He tried to keep himself in the shadows at all times. Out of sight and out of mind. Covert in every aspect of his life. Only a handful of people knew what he did for a living.

Maybe that handful was too big.

"Why did you miss that transmitter earlier?"

"It's a burst transmitter. It only sends a signal every so often. I just managed to catch it tonight."

"Lovely." Her tone was acid. "So much for your phones."

The endless night offered a nearly endless opportunity to consider his screwup and how best to handle it. Then Allie asked the most useful questions of all.

"Tell me, Mr. Genius Bodyguard, why they haven't been on top of us already? Why aren't they here now?"

"I'm working on that."

"Work faster," she said testily.

He kind of liked the way she was reacting. Mad at him, justifiably. Furious about the entire situation. No despair, no tears, no quivering terror. Allie was made of some stern stuff.

"I've been thinking about it," he repeated.

"Then think out loud, for Pete's sake. I'm tired of being a pawn on this chessboard. Move me here, move me there, sit down and shut up like a good girl."

He nearly winced. "I've been doing my job. I didn't intend to be..." He searched for the word.

"Patronizing," she said sharply. "You give a fresh meaning to that word."

"Hell." And this time he didn't keep the cuss to himself.

"Exactly."

A few more cusswords jabbed through his brain but he didn't allow them to pass his lips. Talk about what he was thinking? How he was working through this? Man, did that go against his grain.

But maybe it was time to start rubbing his own grain the wrong way.

"They haven't found us because they can't."

She blew a loud sigh. "You just said we've been transmitting our location."

"Let me finish, please."

She settled, but from the corner of his eye he saw the disapproving way she folded her arms.

"First of all," he said, "I told you it's a *burst* transmitter. It sends a signal every so often. I suspect they didn't think they'd need more than a couple of bursts a day."

"Why not?"

"Because most people drive a straight line, here to there. A couple of those bursts would have told them where we're going. This zigzag route we've been following has prevented that."

For a few beats, she said nothing. "You suspected we could be followed somehow. Or you wouldn't have done this."

"Always expect the worst. Anyway, they probably even thought that when we reached a destination, we'd stay. A few days or more. They'd have us nailed because they'd be right behind us." He paused. "A typical run, they believed. Go hide in another city."

"There's nothing typical about this run," Allie remarked. "Damn."

"We've been confusing them. But they still must have figured out we hit the Pacific Northwest. Maybe they've gotten even closer. That's not good. The transmitter was sending a burst when I found it. They got the location of that lodge."

"Oh, man."

"I also think that in some of the places we've been staying, there was interference with their transmitter. You know, like places where you can't get a cell phone signal. Or even a satellite link. Under thick trees, in the mountains, just to name a few. So there were times they had no idea where we were."

"Then we'd pop up somewhere really weird."

"Yup. Unfortunately nothing is really random, not even me. They've got our general directionality."

"But we're not going anywhere in particular."

"I think it's time we took a drive on a long, straight, fast road. To get away from that lodge. If I missed something, I need to confuse them again. So… It's going to look as if we're headed to Bozeman in Montana. If there's any tracking left that I haven't found, that'll turn their attention that way."

"And then?"

"We're going to turn south into the real middle of nowhere."

"But if they're still tracking somehow?"

"I'm going to stop at a garage along the way. Get this puppy up on a rack and take a good long look."

"And get a new license plate," she said glumly.

"Yup."

Chapter Six

By the time they stopped for a meal, midday had arrived and the area had begun to look more upscale. Christmas lights were so plentiful here that they delighted Allie. After a high-speed drive along a major artery, she wondered when Hale would turn them again. It couldn't be too much longer.

But her eyes felt as if they were full of sand. The medium-sized restaurant offered a varied menu, a pleasant change from the hearty fare at truck stops.

"Christmas," she remarked as they passed under eaves twinkling with icicle lights. The windows were decorated with lighted wreaths and the season had been taken inside with lights running around the ceilings and a toy train making endless circles on a shelf on the wall. "I wonder if I'll miss it completely."

As they sat at a table, Hale spoke. "You have a lot of happy attachments to the season?"

"Yes, I do. Memories that are great. Even after I lost my parents, my aunt and Max would put on a special celebration for me."

"Nice."

"What about you?"

He didn't answer. They were served plenty of piping coffee and plates full of steak. Allie had chosen a baked potato and broccoli but Hale had gone with his usual home fries with a nod to green beans.

"Christmas?" she prodded again.

He looked away, out the window. "Too much drinking and fighting."

"That's awful!"

He shrugged one shoulder. "It was what it was. I guess I shouldn't have answered."

Why? Allie wondered. Because it revealed too much? This guy was a clam. But she'd been right when she had sensed darkness in his past. Being right, however, didn't make her feel even a bit better. She backed away from personal questions, knowing his privacy was important to him.

After a delicious meal, Allie took quite a bit of hers in a carryout box. Despite the feast-or-famine nature of this trip, she still hadn't made the switch to feasting at every opportunity.

Nor did they linger long. All too soon they were back in the car. The drive through Bozeman was pretty, however, and full of evidence that it had become a tourist destination. Ski slopes carved their way up the sides of mountains. The central city, however, had maintained some of its Western appeal.

Suddenly, on the far edge of town, Hale pulled into a parking place. "Stay here," he said. "Keep the doors locked. I won't be long."

She didn't bother arguing. Despite her earlier doubts,

she didn't doubt him now. He was doing his darndest to keep her away from the pursuers, whoever the hell they were.

He was as good as his word, returning less than ten minutes later with a large puffy plastic case and a smaller bag. Once again he threw everything in the back.

"Next the garage."

He was fast there, too. While she watched through the window in the waiting room, in record time Hale got the car up on the pneumatic lift and tires were being changed out while he watched closely. Then he stepped under the vehicle and scanned the entire bottom.

Allie had thought it wasn't allowed for anyone but a mechanic to be under the car, but he must have sweetened the pot somehow.

Half an hour later they were on the road again. He took them four or five exits beyond the populated areas, steered down a ramp and pulled into a rest area.

"Go use the facilities," he suggested. "I'll keep watch out here."

Damn, the place wasn't heated. Not at all. She could have frozen in there.

But a surprise awaited her back at the car. Hale held something in his hands.

"Climb in, Allie."

She slid into the seat, becoming convinced she was going to get pressure sores from it. Then he astonished her.

He unfolded a large burgundy blanket with a Sherpa knit and spread it over her. Next came a neck pillow.

"Hale…"

"It's the least I can do. Get comfy if you can."

It was a whole lot easier now. She settled into warmth and the neck pillow was just right for her.

"Heaven," she said.

"Good."

"What did you mean when you said we're heading for the middle of nowhere?"

"Wyoming cattle country. Almost all of it is grazing land."

She didn't ask why they'd come here if he wanted to go there. She was past that part. In fact, for the first time, she was rooting for this zany drive to continue. That man beside her had piqued her interest. "You didn't find anything more under the car?"

"Not even inside the tires or the rims."

She digested that. "You bought four new tires because of that?"

"Believe it. Although I guess they're *your* tires."

It was only the second time since they'd left that he'd alluded to the fact that this was all on her dime. Even his new tires.

"What are you going to do with them?" she asked wryly. "Try to put them on *my* car? I don't think they'll fit."

"Knock it off my retainer."

Her jaw dropped a bit. Man oh man, had she just insulted him? But she'd agreed to pay all the expenses on this junket and if he felt new tires would help ensure their safety, she wasn't going to cavil.

"Hale, I was just joking."

He didn't answer. Great, she thought. Just great. The stone face was back and not a thing she could do about it.

She scrunched down farther in the soft, warm blanket and finally found a dose of the sleep she'd been needing for a while.

SHE AWOKE AGAIN when she heard gravel beneath the tires. Night had rejoined them, but so had the twinkly lights of a…what? It didn't look like the usual truck stop. Outside the parking lot was plastered mostly with pickup trucks.

"Where are we?" she asked sleepily.

"A roadhouse. And trust me, you don't want to go in there. Stay snuggled under your blanket while I get some food."

"But the steak I saved."

"That's safely flash-frozen somewhere in the back. Keep the doors locked."

The locks *thunked* as he walked away. Even through closed windows she could hear loud country music wailing, and a few of the men smoking on the porch didn't look any too steady. She felt around with her hand and found that crushed hat Hale had given her back in, well, whatever place. She crammed it on her head and pulled it down. As unnoticeable as she could make herself.

The seedier side of the world, although in fairness this was just a bunch of guys out for a good time.

Fifteen minutes later, Hale returned with a couple of handled paper bags. He unlocked the car, climbed in and put the bags behind his seat before taking to the road again.

He spoke. "Fried chicken. Potato salad. Burgers that *have* to be better than any drive-through."

"Any vegetables?"

"Radishes. They go well with beer, I hear. I hope you like them."

"I love them. One year when my mother was planting a garden she said she'd plant any vegetable I wanted. When I asked for radishes, I think she believed I'd lost my mind. But I ate them. Maybe most of them."

He chuckled quietly. "We'll pull over soon so we can eat before everything grows icicles."

"Where are we, Hale? It seems stupid to keep me in the dark now."

"Wyoming mountains. When I find a place for us to sleep, I'll dig out the atlas and show you."

"Thanks for telling me at least what state I'm in. You want to talk about disorientation? I've always liked to know where I am in relation to what. My place on the map."

"I'm not much different. I should have thought about you."

Well, that was a significant admission from him. "This is all so James Bond."

"Hardly," he said drily. "I don't have those fancy cars that can turn into boats and all that."

"True. But it seems we have our own Mr. Big."

"No kidding."

He took a sharp turn onto a dirt road.

"Um…" she began as the trees closed in around them.

"I know where this comes out. Relax."

What choice did she have?

However, it wasn't long before he pulled over and grabbed the bags from the back seat. "A feast," he said. "Sorta."

She was happy to tuck in. All this cold seemed to be making her hungrier, and the fried chicken was some of the best she'd ever eaten. The potato salad, which she ate with a spork, was pretty good, too. And the radishes were crunchy fresh.

They drank bottles of water and for a long time there was no sound except rustling paper, eating and drinking.

"Who invented the spork?" she asked.

"A mad scientist who probably wanted to save plastic."

That pulled a giggle out of her. "Plastics should have gone extinct by now."

"The world would be a happier place if they did. But imagine putting them in zoos to save them."

A real laugh escaped her then. "What an image."

Hale liked hearing her laugh. Maybe she was coming out of despair and her fury with him.

He still had something to figure out, though. What would their pursuers do now?

BUT STU SEEMED to have a pretty good idea where some of them were. At one point or another, his men, according to their training, had placed at least one transmitter on the security guys or Stu wouldn't have been able to tell Hale they were on his tail. Nothing, however, had been said about the whereabouts of the assassin.

Maybe, like Hale, his guys figured the pro was following the security men. Or waiting for them to settle around a particular area. No reason for the killer to follow them all over the place. Waste of his very expensive time.

None of this made Hale happy.

Yeah, surprise.

He'd thought his web of contacts would be able to trace at least one of the security people to a point where he could make Allie safe enough to go after the guy. To question him. To find out something useful against Ellis.

Instead he was going to be facing a pro, much more dangerous to Allie, and a whole lot harder to find.

But Hale *had* to find him. Pros took one shot. If it didn't succeed, they faded away. Until they found another chance.

Stopping that was more important than getting the security men. He'd have other opportunities to get at them. Not so the assassin. One chance, that's all Hale would get.

Unless he wanted to keep Allie on the run for the rest of her life.

Another day. Another six or seven hundred miles. At this rate they were going to run out of Wyoming. He'd replaced the plates again, this time leaving the most recent ones on the truck he'd vandalized.

No trail. Maybe he was getting too good at it this time. Maybe they'd get so far from their pursuers that they could be forgotten for a while. But that wouldn't allow Allie to return to her old life.

Worse, finding that burst transmitter at the lodge last night had made his gut twist. All the running around and zigzagging had been confusing but perhaps ultimately useless.

Eluding the security men for a while had seemed wise. The pro changed all of that. This was no longer about a man or two trying to kidnap Allie at a convenient time and bring her under Ellis's control. Not any longer.

He might never see one of those security men now. He might never know when someone came close enough to tip off the pro unless his guys were successfully tracking them.

That night he found an oddly pink motel back off the road, under the shadows of the trees. He installed Allie in the room he rented, then told her to stay locked inside.

She threw a nightshirt at him but didn't complain. Probably too tired to argue right now. He figured he'd be glad when she grew stubborn again. Part of the real Allie.

Hale was starting to feel exhausted, too. He hadn't been able to catch naps while he was driving, unlike Allie.

Instead he gnawed his insides trying to find a way out of this damn conundrum. On the one hand, he might have done this too well. On the other, he'd screwed up.

But it all came down to making Allie safe for the rest of her life.

He paced around outside for a while, filling his lungs

with sharply cold air. This motel wasn't brightly lighted, and it boasted no Christmas decorations at all. Hanging on by a slim thread, he thought.

Finally, much as he didn't want to, he got a fresh cell and walked to a clearing where the starry sky was visible. Maybe he'd get a signal. Or not. This motel at least had an ancient satellite dish, so some kind of signal had to get through.

Much to his amazement, after walking around the clearing for a bit, he found a strong enough signal. There must be a tower out there somewhere.

Stu answered on the second ring. Not much coded language this time. He simply asked, "What's up?"

"You know where those sous chefs are?"

"Believe it. I've got D and J watching close. Listen, did something happen last night? The wind-up dolls are walking in circles."

"Yeah, I found their remote control."

"Hell, man." Stu fell silent. "You ditched it?"

"Of course." Although not exactly, but no need to reveal that.

"Frick. Sounds like the Keystone Kops."

"I'm not laughing. Keep D and J on it. Knowing where the dolls are…"

"You're right. Well, they started to walk straighter after a couple of hours. Something or someone started to put them in a row. Should we watch out for stairs?"

"Maybe not yet."

Hale rolled back on his heels, staring up at a sky so full of stars that it looked like twinkling diamonds scattered on black velvet.

"Down then sideways," Hale said after a moment. "Not over the edge yet."

"Why?"

"You'll figure it out."

Then Hale stripped the phone and trashed it. The dolls had started to follow a straight line? He wanted to smash more than that phone.

There was a leak, and he didn't know how to plug it. Hell, it might even be an innocent leak.

But it was dangerous regardless.

ALLIE WOKE TO sunshine in the morning. After all these days with Hale she'd grown accustomed to waking in the dark. Sunlight?

She sat bolt upright and saw him sitting in the room's one rickety chair. "What's wrong?"

"We both needed sleep." He rose and stretched. "Take your shower. I'll be waiting outside when you're ready."

As he stood, she smelled the scents of soap and shampoo. Evidently he'd already showered. How had she slept through that?

Napping in the car wasn't enough, she guessed. A long stretch felt good to her, too, as did a nice hot shower. This place might look like a fleabag, but it got a few things right.

Outside, she found Hale pacing. Again she had the feeling that something was wrong but didn't bother to ask. If she'd learned one thing about Hale it was that he wouldn't tell her anything he didn't want to.

After he collected all their bags from the motel room and dropped off the key, he joined her in the car and opened an atlas.

"Wyoming," he said. "Here."

He stabbed at the map with one finger, but at least it gave her a decent idea of their location. The mountains of western Wyoming, slightly to the south of Yellowstone Park.

"I always wanted to go to Yellowstone," she remarked.

"Maybe once we get this sorted out."

Then he tucked the map beneath his seat and they drove away from the pink motel.

ANOTHER SMALL TOWN, this one boasting Christmas ornaments hanging on their few lamp poles. Wreaths in most storefronts. Somehow the attempt seemed half-hearted.

"Christmas," she said again.

"What's with you and Christmas?"

"It's a beautiful time of year. Lots of good memories. I like gathering with my friends, I like the songs and music. There's magic in the air. I hope I don't have to miss it."

Again, no answer. Then she remembered. "Sorry, I guess you have plenty of reason not to feel the same."

After a bit, he said levelly, "Christmas at my house was a war zone. Christmas was when my mother died."

Allie's heart lurched and pain tightened around her chest. "I'm sorry," she murmured thickly.

"Not your fault. Forget I said it."

Forget he said it? Not likely. The picture he'd just painted was heart-wrenching. Wisely, she didn't attempt to say any more.

But now she had plenty to think about. His Christmases had been laced with violence and fighting? His mother had died at Christmas? She felt there was more to the story than he'd ever tell her, but the images of what he had just revealed to her stuck like thistles.

Of course he didn't feel the magic of the holiday season. How could he? Maybe he even hated it. At best he had to be indifferent.

There was no way to change that. Nothing she could say. But one nugget of determination grew in her. There was no way he was going to deprive her of the holiday if there was something she could say about it. Anything she could do.

Because just as he deserved to keep his own attitude, she deserved not to have her own feelings smashed. She had enough smashed already.

Besides, she was so sick of feeling like his duffel bag.

Grimly closing her eyes, she stopped thinking about their pursuers and tried to envision a Currier and Ives Christmas. Something snowy and beautiful and filled with people she liked. A toast of eggnog or mulled cider. Laughter, smiles. Singing whatever carol she chose.

The funny thing about growing up in Southern California was that her only snowy Christmases had been on postcards. But she wanted one anyway. To stand and look up into a dark sky and watch snowflakes fall gently. To feel that added magic surround her. She had long promised herself that she was going to take a trip one year just for the experience.

Now here she was with snow beginning to accumulate around her and sitting with the original Grinch.

At home, her friends would already be planning. Stringing lights and garlands from their balcony rails. JayZee would have put up her artificial tree. She was always the earliest among them. Maybe she was holding her decorating party soon.

The others would be pulling their trees out of storage, some of them predecorated and lighted. Only Kay insisted on a real tree, clinging to it despite the fire hazard because she loved the pine scent that filled her apartment. Allie admitted that she did, too.

Then, of course, all of them would have to help her get rid of the huge tree. Kay couldn't bear having it up after the new year. That was another fun time. After an evening of celebrating the brand-new year, they'd all stand around looking at Kay's tree, their heads aching, and promising they'd get rid of it in a day or two. Not that Kay wanted it gone on New Year's Day, but with hangovers they had a whole lot of fun indulging in a bit of self-pity plus a whole lot of careful laughter.

Boy, she was getting homesick.

She also resolved not to make a deal about Christmas again. Not when the holiday seemed to have so many bad memories for Hale. Keep his mouth shut or else? His mother had died on Christmas Day?

More than bad enough for anyone. She needed to stop pricking him with her desire to have Christmas. Resolved, she kept her mouth shut as they passed through the occasional small town twinkling with lights as if it promised a wonderful day.

When she *did* speak, it was about their current difficulties. "How are you going to find these guys if they can't track us? You got rid of the transmitter, right?"

"I disabled it in case I need it. But otherwise, I'll know where they are, how close they're coming."

Interesting. "Your friends?"

"Yes."

"But how come you don't have *them* take care of this?"

Once again he remained silent, leaving her to wonder.

But Hale knew. He just didn't want *her* to know. The only way he could get this assassin off her tail would be to take him out. Permanently. Bringing in his team would only make matters worse.

He knew the type who took jobs like this. Knew that in order to keep getting hired they had to complete every assignment they took, no matter what was required.

He also knew there'd be no way to get information out of the pro. Zip. If the assassin revealed even a single bit of information, then he'd be on another assassin's target list.

It was a hell of an occupation to get into. It also required a soulless killer. Far worse than a sniper in battle who at least had a reason other than money and the thrill of a kill.

He remembered one aging SEAL he'd known, a

sniper who'd been active in Vietnam. He'd talked about a great many things that he'd never forgotten, but one was branded in his brain and haunted him constantly. The time the man had taken out a Vietcong general as he sat on a porch with his family.

Some things could never be forgotten, not if you had a soul, a heart, a conscience. The type who was after Allie possessed none of that Being able to take out a target at a kilometer was the least of it.

Hale also hoped the guy didn't have a spotter to aid his calculations on the shot, which would limit his target range. Or that he couldn't get a clear line of sight, which would force him in closer.

A lot to hope for, although the use of a spotter was highly unlikely. These assassins worked alone, counting on experience, without help with important matters, such as wind drift, air temperature and density, even the movement of the earth over a sufficient distance. Or the movement of the target. No decent sniper fired in a straight line.

So the pro would have to come in reasonably close, which made him a much easier target for Hale. Still, even with a hunting rifle, a sniper could be deadly over two hundred yards.

Nor would there be a red dot on the target the way the movies showed. Laser sights were useless except at very close range, such as with a pistol.

Even so, the red dot, despite movies, wouldn't give the target time to move out of the way. A bullet came fast enough that dodging to one side, or even falling to the knees, wouldn't be fast enough. By the time the dot was sighted, it would be too late. A bullet would already be on its way at supersonic speed.

Hell's bells. Thinking all this over wasn't making Hale feel any better.

Yeah, the sniper would have constraints, but would they be enough?

Hale mulled over the problem as the miles slipped away. He also made a point of avoiding any clear lines of sight. Trees and irregular movements made damn good cover.

Then he noticed that Allie wasn't mentioning Christmas any longer. Damn, had he done that to her?

That ought to remind him to keep his mouth shut.

ALLIE WAS BUSY trying not to think about anything at all. Using every meditative technique she'd ever learned wasn't helping.

Brains just never shut up.

Her thoughts insisted on returning to the friends she missed. To Christmases past. To gifts she had wrapped and that waited in her closet for Christmas Eve. About the gifts she'd bought to donate to children, from the Angel Tree to Toys for Tots.

"Hale," she said, breaking her silence for the first time in hours, "do you know about the Angel Tree?"

"No." No question followed.

She decided to tell him anyway. "The tree is covered with little paper angels. On the back of each is written a gift some child wishes for, along with age and gender."

"Okay."

"Of course, there are the usual. You can't keep a middle schooler from wanting a video game."

Hale snorted. "No kidding."

"But then there are the ones that just break your heart. A four-year-old who wants a jacket. Another little kid who just wants a pair of shoes. Nothing about an expensive athletic shoe, just shoes."

"Hell."

"Yeah. Plenty of kids live in it. Anyway, when I'd come across those I'd put the item in a big holiday bag and then add a large teddy bear, something to make a kid smile."

"Joy."

"I always hoped so." Deciding he wasn't totally opposed to this discussion of the holiday, she continued. "There was a church nearby that had a congregation that was mostly migrants. That was a different kind of shopping expedition. Lots of large bags of rice and beans. Canned goods. School supplies. So much need out there."

He didn't answer immediately. Then he said, "You have a good heart."

"I don't know about that. I'm just *aware*. I've been lucky my entire life. How can I ignore the fact that's not true for everyone?"

"Lots of people seem to get by doing exactly that."

"Unfortunately." She sighed quietly, leaning back onto the neck pillow. "Mostly I just felt I never did enough. Anyway, I have stuff for the Angel Tree and Toys for Tots. I hope one of my friends remembers that and pulls them out of my closet."

"I'm sure they will." So someone else had a key to her apartment? That made him uneasy. Another target for questioning?

God, this black hole just kept getting deeper. He had to finish this soon.

Chapter Seven

Even for Hale, the days had begun to run together. Endlessly the same.

Until several nights later when he checked in with Stu.

"I don't know what happened, man," Stu said. "But the dolls seem to have direction. I don't know if they're headed toward you or what."

Hale felt everything inside him tighten. "Where?" he asked.

"Better question is how close." Stu waited.

Hale no longer had any intention of sharing his position, however vaguely. The idea of a traitor among men he had believed to be his friends was getting stronger. Right then the feeling was pinging him like a transmitter.

"Stu," he said. Nothing more.

"Yeah. I'm wondering. I'm working on it."

"And the dolls?"

"I heard they were bought by a store near Bozeman."

Hale's stomach knotted so tightly that it felt as if it had been stabbed. "Not anymore," he said, revealing his concern. "They passed through on their way to another retailer."

Stu swore a long stream. Loudly and vociferously as only a battle-hardened veteran could do. "I get it. I want the whole damn collection, and the collector, too. This was supposed to be a present for my godchild."

"Nice to know why they got sold in the first place."

"Can't trust anybody, it seems."

It certainly did. Hale began to run a mental check of his entire network. "I'll think about it."

"You're not the only one."

So the security men had followed them all the way to Bozeman. How? And Stu had no idea where the hit man was. Not yet.

The only way this could get worse would be waking up in the morning with a gun barrel in his face.

Hale dumped another phone on another truck, then took Allie inside for a hot meal. She must be sick of roadside diners and this place claimed to be something more. Breakfast around the clock. Considering the number of vehicles outside, he hoped that was a recommendation.

Inside, the charm oozed but the diners looked happy and chatted like it. He and Allie found their way to a table away from the windows. He might be a fool about his friends, but he wasn't a fool about precautions.

The four-page menu was breakfast end to end. Allie surprised him by ordering pancakes and breakfast sausage. Soon a thermal carafe of coffee sat between them along with bottles of three kinds of syrup.

"Nothing to go with that?" he asked. He expected her to be scouring the pages for veggies of any kind.

"If I'm going to misbehave, I might as well do it up."

For once he smiled. "Enjoy."

"Oh, I intend to."

When the server returned with their order, she added a small cheese-and-potato casserole.

He exceeded her indulgence only by quantity and by the fact that he preferred ham to breakfast sausage. He also made a private bet with himself that she wouldn't eat half of what she had ordered.

She spoke during their pigout. "I was able to go to college on my dad's insurance. His union helped a bit with it, too. But I felt guilty as sin for doing it."

"I'm sure that's what he hoped you'd do."

"Maybe. But it was like taking blood money."

Oh, for Pete's sake, he thought. Blood money? She didn't understand the term, but he let it slide for now.

"Anyway, despite everything, I enjoyed myself. It was a great time. It was also the first time I realized that my entire future was ahead of me and that I could do anything I chose with it."

"That must have felt heady."

"It did. For a while."

He tilted his head to one side. "But?"

"I made all the usual mistakes. Boyfriends for one. They're a great sidetrack to get on."

"Off the rails?" he asked.

"Easily. I still remember the day I broke up with one of them. I wasn't brokenhearted."

He nodded. "Okay."

"I felt relieved. Totally relieved. As if I were getting my life back."

An interesting reaction, he thought.

"You ever break up with anyone and feel better for it?"

Her question deserved an honest answer, much as he hated revealing himself. He took a moment to eat another mouthful of nicely browned ham before he spoke.

"I think I felt that way most of the time."

Allie raised both brows. "No broken heart?"

"I never let myself get that involved."

ALLIE HAD PLENTY to think about that after they started driving again. Never let himself get that involved?

He was more than a monolith of silence. Apparently he was locked up so deep inside himself that feelings rarely surfaced. What the hell had done that to him?

She expected no answers, not from him. Which gave her reason to speculate. Except that the only thing she really knew about him was that his mother had died on Christmas and that there'd been a lot of fighting. Could that have been enough to shut him down?

Maybe so. Maybe so. But she'd lost both her parents and hadn't closed herself off. She enjoyed all the memories.

Something else was going on.

HALE KEPT WAITING for it. He'd said too much about his relationships with women. She was bound to want to know why. Even he understood that no one would consider it natural. And Allie didn't always hesitate to tread where angels feared to go.

But he hated her questions because they kept drawing bits of himself into the open. Bits he really didn't want to share.

But he couldn't bring himself to lie to her, not directly. Except by omission, because it was necessary, but not to one of her point-blank questions when he couldn't see an honest way around it.

Winter was growing deeper, at least to judge by the amount of snow he was beginning to see alongside the road, from the way snow and ice now blanketed the pavement. Here they were, heading south into what appeared to be the remains of a blizzard.

How very unfortunate. It was slowing him down more than he otherwise would have needed on this curvy road.

But they were making their way through trees, and most roads like this happened for a reason. They tended to be built along tracks that had been used for a long time, not just built for no reason at all. Someone had traveled this way countless times over the years.

Then a house seemed to pop out of nowhere, surrounded by dozens of blue-lighted artificial holiday trees, by clear lights strung around evergreens and along bare branches, by multicolored lights hanging from the edge of the roof. It seemed totally overdecorated for a dwelling so isolated.

Then he glimpsed Allie's face. Her expression had softened, a faint dreamy smile curving her mouth. He slowed down even more, allowing her to drink in the scene. Christmas. She wanted her Christmas.

He could smell a burst of stubbornness coming. The only question was how he would deal with it.

After the house had disappeared into the darkening woods, Allie remarked, "You said you had a wife."

He tried to remember telling her that, then recalled the tossed-off answer to her question. "It was a cover story. You asked how I'd justify buying women's clothes."

"Oh."

Yeah. *Oh.* He'd told her he didn't get involved, so naturally she summoned that from the depths of her memory. And he'd believed that he'd learned to keep his mouth shut. Not tight enough, evidently.

As the darkness deepened even more, he turned them onto an eastbound road. He hoped he'd get a clue from Stu about how closely they were being followed.

Allie spoke again, miles later. "You said your mother died on Christmas."

"So?" He hoped he made the word forbidding enough that she wouldn't pursue the issue.

She either didn't get it or didn't want to get it.

"How did it happen?"

His hands tightened on the steering wheel until they hurt. Then rage hit him and he poured the sewer on her.

"My dad was a drunk. A terrible drunk. He'd beat my mother over nothing. Hell, he beat me, too. We lived in fear, always tiptoeing around. Trying not to get his attention. That didn't work. It didn't help when he'd apologize the next morning. He didn't mean to do it, he said. But he taught me to keep my mouth shut. He didn't want to hear a word from me."

"Oh my God," she murmured.

"A lot of children grow up with that. Nothing unusual." *Let it go, Allie. Just let it go.*

"That doesn't make what you endured any better."

"No." Nothing made it better.

"And your mother?" This time she spoke tentatively.

But he was past caring. Rage still held him in its thrall. He could have told her nothing. He could have refused to answer, but fury pushed him.

"Then, when I was twelve, he beat my mother to death on Christmas Day. I tried to stop him but he hit me so hard I could barely breathe. Then I tried again anyway and he kicked me in the head and broke my jaw. I was afraid he'd kill me. So I didn't move, didn't try again. I cowered in a corner while he beat and kicked my mother to death."

"Oh, Hale…"

"I never saw him again after that. He went to prison. Too late."

"And you?"

"Foster home." He bit off the words and at last she stopped pressing him. Still, she'd brought the memories to the forefront, a place he tried to never let them go. He saw red and probably should have stopped driving. He drove too fast for the road conditions.

Finally he shoved the memories back into the black hole where he tried to keep them. One way or another, they'd played a part in making him the man he was, and that man was trying to save a young woman's life.

This fight had become personal.

ALLIE NOW HAD more to think about than she wanted. A mind filled with images she'd never seen herself, but images she had no trouble filling in.

God, that any kid should be treated that way. That any kid should see his mother beaten to death.

She knew it happened, of course, but she refused to follow such stories in the news. Playing ostrich because it was hard to deal with such things. Because it made her heart hurt.

Now her heart was hurting for the man beside her. Now she knew why he was so silent and she couldn't criticize him for it.

She shouldn't have pressed him like that. She should have practiced some silence herself. But the desire to know Hale better was growing inside her like a force of its own.

As annoyed as she got with him putting her through this endless trip, she didn't hate him. She'd never hated him. He just drove her nuts. Then she'd pierced his brick wall of self-protection. Well, she'd gotten exactly what she deserved, an ugly, angry explanation she'd never be able to erase from her memory. As he probably couldn't.

She wanted to apologize for her trespass but decided that could be dangerous. He'd just remember his father's apologies, apologies that had meant nothing. Apologies that hadn't prevented his mother's death.

She was relieved when he slowed the SUV down. Yeah, she'd been worried about their speed, but not as upset as she was by what he'd revealed. He must be sitting beside her feeling like a raw nerve. Angry with her for pushing him into memory.

Why had he even answered her prying? He could have told her it was none of her business. Although she had to admit she probably wouldn't have given up.

People called her stubborn, even Max, but she was more persistent than stubborn. Or so she'd always believed. Persistence had gotten her a long way.

But maybe others were right. Maybe it was cussedness on her part. Her dad had always said so when faced with it.

What did it matter what she called it? She'd done it, she shouldn't have, and now they both had to live with the results.

It wasn't as if she could change her personality in an instant or two. But maybe that was a lousy excuse. Especially this time.

A while later, she changed tack. "Max is okay, right?"

"Max knows how to take care of himself. Ellis isn't the first bad guy he's had to deal with. He's probably got his whole team on alert."

She hoped so. "I'm worrying more about him than me."

"Ellis makes one wrong move and Max will be all over him like white on rice. Max is just waiting for a chance and Ellis probably knows it. What's more, he doesn't want to stir the hornet's nest that would come from attacking a cop."

"That's a good point." And it was. Several times in her life she'd seen how cops reacted to one of their number being hurt or killed. They wouldn't let go until they had the perp.

"But you and Max said Ellis is too insulated."

"Maybe. But one little mistake…"

He left the statement unfinished. It hung on the air like a threat. Maybe it was.

"You really think you're going to be able to take care of Ellis?"

Hale's response was flat and cold. "Or die trying."

Allie subsided, thinking about the man who was escorting her to safety. She hadn't been wrong when she had decided he was dangerous.

HALE STARTED TO feel awful about dumping on Allie. All his life he'd remained silent about what he'd seen. Even when social services insisted he see a counselor, even though his foster family had tried to get him to open up, he'd never said a word. Not once. Not even when it might have helped.

Instead he'd focused on a career that would force him to face down fear, that would make him physically strong enough to deal with men like his father.

A job that would forever prevent him from cowering in a corner.

At twelve there hadn't been much he could have done to save his mother. They didn't even have a phone so he could call for help. Not that he could have talked after his jaw was broken.

But that wasn't what truly troubled him. He'd hated himself for that cowardice. Even if he couldn't take on the beast who had sired him, it was the cowardice that stuck with him.

The Marines had taught him something useful, however. Everyone felt fear. If you didn't feel fear there was something wrong with you. But you had to face the fear. That was the birth of all bravery. Facing the fear and not giving in to it.

The man he was today never would have let that bastard beat his mother. He wouldn't have been afraid to open his mouth. He wouldn't have lived in terror or allowed his mother to.

No, he'd have decked that SOB as many times as were necessary to drive him from the house. His father would have been the one cowering.

But he still hated that twelve-year-old. He still felt guilty. He couldn't even find forgiveness in his heart for that kid. The boy had failed miserably. Seriously. Horribly.

He'd transformed himself. He worked now to save people. Maybe that helped make up for some of his past. He didn't know. He could only hope.

Hope was a slender thread.

Chapter Eight

As the middle of the night arrived, while he kept an eye out for a motel, Hale became acutely aware that Allie hadn't spoken in hours.

Huddled in the corner of the passenger seat, she was silent. And he didn't think she was sleeping.

He cleared his throat. Something needed saying. Instead of remaining comfortable in his silence, as he usually did, he began to feel badly.

"I shouldn't have dumped on you."

She stirred at last. "I'm glad you did."

Glad? *Glad?* She was losing her mind, hardly surprising after this journey he'd kept her on. But having been followed at least to Bozeman, he no longer felt even moderately safe only because he believed there was no longer a transmitter on the car.

Not even keeping mostly to roads with tree cover, or roads surrounded by mountains, felt like enough to make Allie safe.

Damn, he had to nail this Ellis guy. Put a stop to his killings. Put a stop to *him*.

He spoke again. "Men like Ellis."

When he didn't continue, she prompted him. That was Allie, never let it go.

"Men like Ellis," he continued. "They shouldn't be able to sit safely atop their billions twisting the law with their batteries of lawyers. Things that would get an ordinary man convicted of felonies, of frauds, maybe of murder, skate by without a worry."

"I can't disagree with that. But I never saw him that way."

"Almost nobody does. But you remember that kid who couldn't save his mother? Too afraid? Well, Ellis has that kind of grip on too many people in his organization. When he needs to warn them, he does. All without it tracing back to him."

"God, you make him sound like one of those villains on TV or in the movies."

"Yup. And he is. He's not the only one, either. The world is full of men with his resources who never face any real legal threat. Or consequences."

Which left her chewing on thoughts that had nothing to do with his past. That was fine with him, because he didn't want to face any more questions about his childhood. More cowardice? Maybe, but this time he didn't care.

As they reached a large clearing, the moon emerged in a clear-as-crystal sky. Full now, it cast its silvery light on the world below, creating a snow glow that was brighter than the moon itself.

Then he spied a turnout that he suspected had been dug by a plow changing direction. He pulled over, thinking Allie would at least get a chance to stretch.

He needed one himself and, cold or not, it would make them both feel better.

"Let's take a breather," he said as he switched off the ignition.

She nearly leaped at the opportunity. She was out of the car before he could come around the front to her side. Her head tipped back as she looked up at the full moon, as she inhaled deep breaths and blew large clouds on each exhalation.

"Take it easy on those deep breaths," he said. "They'll chill you much faster."

She surprised him with a laugh, then spun around with her arms extended. "We should stay here tonight."

"Well, if we had polar sleeping bags, and a tent…"

She laughed again. "I know. We'd be frozen peep-sicles before long."

He couldn't resist and laughed with her.

"It's still a lovely thought," she added, lowering her arms and looking around. "Much better than those motel rooms. Are you picking the worst ones or what?"

"Very downscale," he admitted. "People coming through those places are nearly invisible. You'd be surprised how rarely they want me to register."

"Maybe I wouldn't be. As near as I can tell, you have the corner on being covert."

He wished he had, but he didn't disagree. "I think it helps that I pay in cash. I suspect it doesn't get reported as income."

She paused, then said, "I guess a lot of those places are barely hanging on. I wouldn't blame them."

She turned more slowly this time, taking in the entire

clearing, the snow-laden branches of the evergreens that encircled it. "It's perfect," she breathed. "Just perfect."

He spied a game trail just beyond the snow that had been mounded by the plow. He pointed it out.

"Do you see it? The game trail?"

She moved forward a little. "Oh, yes! What do you think comes through there? And why? For what?"

"Food mostly, whether they're browsers or carnivores. Maybe there's a water source that hasn't frozen over yet, although I imagine the larger animals, like elk, could break it open, helping out everyone else."

"I like that idea." A smile filled her face, and Hale thought the sight of Allie enjoying something could become addictive. She asked, "Bears are hibernating right now?"

"Sort of."

"What's that mean?"

"They come out of their dens every so often to browse."

"I never knew that!"

Another wave of delight filled her face. "But I bet life is tough right now for most animals."

"Except beavers."

She faced him, her expression disbelieving. "In frozen streams and ponds? How could they be better off?"

"Beavers are the original good neighbors. They spend all their time until winter building their dams and filling them with food. Planning ahead. But then, this will amaze you, other little animals find their ways in. And the beavers let them stay all winter and eat from the food supply."

"Wow." She drew another deep breath of the fresh

air. "Imagine if we were all like that. Think we'll see any animals come along here?"

He smiled faintly. "Not likely. They'd want to avoid us. Anyway, the full moon messes up their rhythms."

"How'd you come to learn so much about this?"

"It interests me. I don't spend *all* my time dragging young women all over the place."

"From nowhere to the middle of nowhere."

Hale gestured to the surrounding area. "The middle of nowhere can be a wonderful place."

It wasn't long before he urged her back into the car. He saw the small shivers she was trying to repress. Time to warm her up.

He was damn glad he'd been able to share those minutes with her.

ALLIE TOOK A while to warm up, even wrapped in the blanket Hale had given her, remembering the clearing with a sense of magic.

She dozed fitfully until the sun rose well in the sky. She stirred, clearing her throat, reaching for one of the bottles of water Hale kept stashed behind the passenger seat. After she downed a half bottle, she asked, "Where was our motel? Did I sleep through it?"

"Time to alter the routine. We'll stop soon and spend a day sleeping instead of a night."

"I can probably do that." She tried and failed to stifle a yawn.

"I'm sure we both can. I'll try to find a place where you can walk around."

"I'd love that. But why always these out-of-the-way places? I mean, there's rarely a town around."

"The more places you're seen, the easier…"

"To identify me from a photo. I remember. But I don't look much like my old self, starting with my hair. You know, I still resent that. My hair was my best feature."

"If you believe that, then you need a new mirror."

She supposed that was meant as a compliment, although given her experience of Hale, she wondered if there were other ways it could be taken. He didn't at all seem like a man who paid compliments. In fact, given that he hardly talked, he probably wouldn't know how to summon one.

With her head turned sideways on her neck pillow, she studied him, wishing he'd get rid of that beard, which was getting too long for her taste. Too long period. He was well on his way to resembling one of those scruffy reality TV stars.

On the other hand. Yeah, on the other hand. Chiseled cheeks, a strong forehead, a thick hairline. When her attention was drawn to his mouth, *she* was drawn to some pretty hot thoughts.

And that body. One glimpse of him wrapped in a towel had remained engraved on her brain. She didn't have to wonder what was under that green jacket or those jeans. Or even under the flannel shirts he usually wore.

Sighing, she turned her head back to look out the window. He might be eye candy, but he was dangerous in so many ways. Trying to get close to him would probably singe off her wings.

Midmorning, just about the time Allie thought she'd throw a hissy if she couldn't escape this car, Hale apparently saw a so-called motel that appealed to him.

Just as he was getting out of the car to get the room, she said, "I should warn you now. If there's anything crawling in that room, I'm going to throw a fit."

"I wouldn't blame you."

"I'm serious, Hale. I don't want to stay here." She felt her chin stick out stubbornly. Naturally, he just ignored her protest.

He'd probably spent some time on the ground with many things that crawled, given his Marine background. She doubted he'd shrink from a roach.

But *she* would. "I've stayed in better places that had a critter problem."

"What made you bring this up? You've never said anything like this before."

She cocked an eye at the building. "There's something about this place."

"At least it's not the Bates Motel."

Which was probably intended to make her laugh, but it failed. She didn't need a Norman Bates to make her scream in the shower.

No, creepy-crawlies could bring her to her knees. She'd once hired an exterminator to take care of one spider. Well, spiders could have more than two hundred babies at a time. She felt as if the insides of her walls were crawling just from seeing that one ugly thing. A *furry* one, for heaven's sake.

The exterminator had agreed with her, probably justifying his charge, but nothing could stir her from her conviction. And nothing could make her comfortable with parts of the insect universe.

But why this motel was the first to give her the willies she didn't know. She hadn't *liked* most of them, but she hadn't thought about bugs.

Maybe this constant flight was driving her mad. For real. But there didn't seem to be a way out of it, not when Max had said she should run, not when Hale kept following his crazy path and talking about pursuers being too close.

Most especially when he'd found a transmitter on the car.

It was still hard to believe anyone wanted her that badly. Hard to believe the error she'd found in Ellis's books couldn't just be fixed by auditors. Just something out of balance. Just a few payouts overlooked. Dealing with a business so complex, things happened.

It should have ended there. She'd reported it, he could fix it. But evidently no one thought Ellis would be content with that.

She must have found the tip of an iceberg of some kind. Or the loose thread on a sweater that should never be pulled.

She might feel a bit better about all of this mess if she had at least known how she'd set it in motion.

She saw Hale come out of the office, but instead of heading directly to the car, he let himself into one of the rooms. He'd never done that before. Did he feel like he might have met Norman Bates after all?

Growing increasingly edgy, she waited for ten minutes until he returned. He knocked on her window and she rolled it down, feeling the blast of frigid air.

"All inspected, Allie. No bugs."

"Thank you," she answered with as much dignity as she could muster, given that she now felt incredibly embarrassed.

"It's okay," he said with a gentleness that totally amazed her. She'd never heard anything approaching that tone from him.

"I shouldn't have made such a big deal out of it." Although her feeling had been strong.

"I said it's okay." He leaned in a little. "People have phobias. They're not a choice. Anyway, I don't think either of us wants to spend all day trying to desensitize you."

"No," she admitted, horrified by the thought.

"It wouldn't work anyway."

Which left her wondering just what he meant. She seemed to do a lot of that with Hale.

But that gentleness in his voice… Dang, she couldn't let that tug at her battered feelings. She couldn't allow herself to be attracted to him. She tried to tell herself that she didn't even like him.

Besides, he worked for her. She didn't want to be guilty of sexual harassment, even inadvertently.

Or did she?

The question brought a small smile to her lips as she trudged her way across snow behind Hale, who carried their duffels.

HALE WONDERED IF Allie had the least idea how she revved his motor as she exercised on the dubious floor. He'd spread out towels for her to keep her from feeling icky, then went to the office and got another stack for their showers.

So he got the full view of her bottom cased in the softer pants he'd bought for her. The sight made him pause on the threshold, then he quickly corralled himself.

Nope, absolutely not. His desires right then hardly qualified as protection. The more so since she was in his charge.

But he enjoyed a savory moment of self-indulgence.

Ah, well. He eased around her and stacked the towels on the bathroom sink. He felt no desire to fuss with hanging them on the rack.

Then he went to the little sink in the bedroom to take advantage of the small coffee maker and one of the two packets of some kind of cheap coffee. At least it smelled good while it brewed.

"Want some?" he asked when she finished her workout. "Or will it keep you awake?"

"It would take a nuclear explosion to keep me awake," she retorted. "Oh, wait, that would only be for a split second."

"Coffee?" he repeated as he smothered a grin.

"Please. After my shower."

When she sat on the edge of the single bed with her hair wrapped in a towel, he brought her coffee.

"They always say those things make four cups," he remarked.

"And it's never more than two."

He took the one creaky chair near the window. "I'm going to make a call in a little while."

"Okay. Getting more information?"

"I hope something useful." If those guys had gotten any closer, he wanted to know how they'd managed. "Soon I might make use of that last transmitter I found."

She turned a bit on the bed so she could look at him more directly. "What will that do?"

"It'll send some bursts headed a long way from us."

She nodded approvingly. "Good idea. But don't we have to let them get close?"

He didn't want to go there because he could imagine all the ideas she'd throw up at him, every one of which would put her in danger. Then she'd give him hell when he wouldn't cooperate.

"Not yet," he said. "Not until I'm ready."

"When's that going to be? The twelfth of never?"

He didn't respond. What was the point? He had to be sure one of the security guys was close enough that the pro would probably be nearby. He needed to find out when the hunters tapered off to just one or two in the same area. For that he needed Stu.

This situation was beginning to frustrate him beyond belief. He'd had good reasons for taking Allie on the run, but the determined tracking, the hiring of a hit man, more than concerned him.

He'd cherished the faint hope that Ellis would give up when he couldn't find her. That he'd give up when he realized she'd gone too far away to make trouble for him. That all this skipping around would make the task look damn near impossible.

All he'd wanted was to get his hands on one of the security men to interrogate him. The hit man brought everything to a new level.

A much more dangerous level. Even if the security men gave up, the pro wouldn't. Not ever. So the assassin needed the goons Ellis had sent as bloodhounds, because there was no way the hit man would waste his time without leads.

Someone had to be guiding them toward Allie. The question plaguing him was who or what. The growing worry was that he might not know in time that trouble was on them.

He began to consider ways to make Allie safe while he went on a hunt of his own.

Maybe that illegal ID wasn't such a bad idea after all. She needed to be able to rebuild her life, and she wasn't going to do it at home unless he totally demolished the threat.

Allie would lose too much, beginning with her friends. Like going into witness protection, she'd have to cut all ties with everyone and everything in her past.

He couldn't stand the thought of doing that to her. He wouldn't wish that on anyone, except possibly a hardened criminal.

"Heard a funny true story," he said in answer to a silence from her that was beginning to be weighted with despair or anger.

"Yeah?" she asked quietly.

"Yeah. Big-time criminal squealed on the mob. He

was put into witness protection but it seemed he couldn't mend his ways. In a new town, a new city, he started running scams."

Now she sounded interested. "Some nerve."

"That's what the local police thought. Five times they arrested him, and five times the Marshals stepped in, demanding the charges be dropped because they'd reveal the guy's identity and he'd be at risk for his life."

"Tell me they got rid of him!"

"Sure did. The fifth time the cops arrested him, they ignored the Marshals' pleas. They not only charged him but shared his identity, old and new, with a reporter. The local paper couldn't resist a scoop like that."

"I should hope not."

He was relieved to see that she was smiling again. "Anyway, the Marshals had to scoop the guy up and move him. And thus the cops cleared the idiot from their town and all local areas."

"That must have been a relief."

"I bet it was. Enough that the chief did an interview with the paper, telling them about all the times the Marshals stepped in."

"Does anyone deserve that much protection?" She shook her head.

"Some do." Then he rose. "I'm going to make that call now."

She shook her head again. "At least this time tell me something about it. I hate living in the dark."

"I'll do what I can." But he wasn't going to promise anything. He knew better than that. Allie would never let him off the hook.

Her stubbornness was returning, too. Of course it was. She was beginning to find her stability in this new way of living.

Trouble was brewing from more than one direction.

Stu answered on the second ring. Hale came right to the point.

"News?"

"Headed south on Ninety-Five."

Everything in Hale tensed into steel. "Why?" he demanded.

"When did I become a mind reader? This a problem?"

But Hale refused to reveal his whereabouts or that the goons seemed to be following a parallel path. Someone knew too much and he didn't know who. "Odd way for them to turn," he said instead.

"Been thinking about that," Stu replied. "I think the big-city route is being followed. Next is Cheyenne. Unlikely to think you headed east into the Badlands, or something."

So Stu was giving thought to Hale's whereabouts, too. Uneasiness pricked Hale. Stu couldn't be the traitor. Not Stu. For God's sake, he'd saved the man's life.

But there were other guys working this job. Other guys who might have found an incentive to provide info to Ellis's cronies. Other men he'd trusted but who might be thinking hard about where Allie was.

"Cheyenne isn't that big a city," he remarked, then waited for the answer.

"Isn't it the capital?"

"I'm not sure." Providing no real information. "Not that there are a whole lot of people in that general area." For a fact, Wyoming was a huge state, land-wise, but populated by around six hundred thousand people. It made sticking to the boonies so much easier. "Anyway, there are fewer in the Badlands." Stick that in your craw, Stu.

"I would have thought you'd be looking for a busy place by now."

Seeking information. Hale ground his teeth. Not Stu. "How many are you still tracking?"

"Two."

Which meant either that Hale's network had lost the trail of the rest, or that Ellis had called them back as extraneous. Now, why would Ellis think that?

It felt odd to be talking to Stu in the light of day. "I've been on too long," he said, then disconnected. This time he put the phone, battery removed, in his lock box. No poor person was going to carry it all over the hinterlands. Not this time. Something had to be pinging them, and he was beginning to distrust his phones, despite all the precautions he'd taken.

"Well, hell," he announced to the universe. "Just damn it all to hell."

He looked up into the blue overhead, wondering about eyes in the sky. Could Ellis actually be following them by satellite? But if he was, wouldn't his henchmen be closer to Hale and Allie than they were? Or maybe he kept losing track of them because of Hale routing them through trees.

Could the guy actually get that much time on a satellite? Pay for it, yes, but get the time?

Maybe he needed to find an out-of-sight place to spray-paint his vehicle.

Or maybe his skills weren't as sharp as he'd thought.

When he reentered the room, Hale felt like his hands were going to fall off. He should have worn his gloves.

Allie slept soundly in the bed, so he settled quietly on the floor to sleep.

Except that he couldn't. He closed his eyes, but his mind was in hyperdrive, buzzing like angry bees, wondering how best to guard against this new threat, whatever it was. Maybe traveling at night would be best now. Finding a place to go to ground in the daylight.

Unless, of course, Ellis was getting infrared images as well from that possible satellite. Hale's car's engine would show up like a beacon any hour of the day or night.

What if he hadn't been as canny with those phones as he thought? He'd learned the methods from an electronics security expert, but that didn't mean he'd learned everything. Or that phones hadn't somehow changed. Or that algorithms for pinging them hadn't changed.

He rolled on his side, ignoring the concrete underflooring and the pressure it put on his shoulder. Light still streamed between the curtains, allowing him to see the puffy bundle that Allie had become.

She needed her rest. She needed to be comfortable. She needed a whole bunch of things he couldn't provide on this road trip from hell.

So far he'd evaded their pursuers, but now they were

getting closer. Allie was right, that day needed to come so he could deal with it and set her free.

But she couldn't be in the middle of it. Absolutely not. He'd have to stash her safely somehow. Out here, places to stash her weren't thick on the ground.

He closed his eyes, telling himself to catch a nap. As a soldier he'd learned to sleep whenever and wherever he could.

That was another skill that seemed to be eluding him.

Chapter Nine

Hale lugged them out of the motel just after twilight. Allie still seemed groggy after her long sleep.

"Food next," he said.

"Yeah, this place is just brimming with restaurants."

Well, she hadn't lost her bite, groggy or not. Once again he smothered a smile. This woman was getting under his skin and he enjoyed her bursts of attitude.

Much more entertaining than most of the people he'd protected. But... She had stopped mentioning Christmas, and he was sure that was his fault. He should never have let the dam break and spill *his* Christmas story.

Well, it was done. He couldn't take it back now.

"I'm sorry I can't take you to better restaurants."

"Oh, for heaven's sake, Hale. We're on the run. I don't have to like it."

"True," he agreed. "One more greasy spoon coming up."

She snorted. Had that sound just escaped her ladylike mouth? "Did you learn anything last night?"

Back to his phone call. What should he tell her and how much? He had to keep her on this road trip, but he didn't want her threatening to stand her ground. That would be one headache too much.

"Well," he said carefully, "they're moving south from Bozeman. Maybe on the way to Cheyenne."

She said nothing for a few beats, then asked, "Are we headed that way?"

"At the moment we're heading west. All good so far."

"But they have to come closer, don't they? You've got to catch them, right?"

Back to this again. His answer was blunt. "Not until I'm ready to stop them."

"Oh, for…" She stopped. "How the heck will you know?"

"I just will. Trust my battle sense."

"I've been trusting you a whole hell of a lot."

"I know you have." *Let it lie, Allie. Just leave it.*

But she didn't. Naturally. "How do they even know what state we're in?"

"I'm working on that. In the meantime, I planted a false clue. We'll see if they react accordingly."

"And somehow that's supposed to get us free of them?"

"Not exactly." But it would sure give him some idea of how they were being tracked. Whether someone in his intelligence network had sold them out. The very thought made his gut twist.

"Seriously, Hale, why not just bring them in right now?"

"Because I choose my own place and time." His tone foreclosed further discussion, and he guessed she heard it.

Funny how her silence could be louder than her words. If she hadn't already, she was going to drive some guy nuts. He wouldn't mind watching.

Then she punctured the ice. "Am I a pain, Hale?"

"Only when you choose to be."

"Such a diplomatic answer," she retorted tartly. "Probably as close to the truth as you get."

"I never lie."

"Only by omission. And there are plenty of those."

He couldn't deny it. He was glad to see a diner ahead. Stuck out in the middle of nowhere, probably supported by ranchers and hired hands who didn't have the time or the money to head for bright city lights.

The parking lot was only half-plowed, the rest fairly mashed by tires. There was hardly anyone in the lot, however. He'd have preferred the place to be busy, providing more cover. On the other hand, in places like this people tended to be tight-lipped with outsiders.

Inside, the establishment boasted age-roughened plank floors, wood walls covered with beer signs and photos that seemed to be of rodeo stars. The country music that played was of an earlier generation.

The menu was a big painted sign over the lunch counter. Despite the neon beer signs, there was no bar. If you wanted a drink, it had to be beer.

Allie looked around, then moved to a table away from the window.

"You want something to drink? I'd be surprised if there isn't coffee."

"Just water, please."

He went to the counter and got himself a coffee and her glass of water. None of the bottled stuff here.

"Have you had a chance to scan the menu?" he asked.

"Such as it is. Not yet."

He couldn't blame her. There wasn't a whole lot to choose from and he was almost surprised there wasn't some kind of blue plate special. People of extremely moderate means must patronize the place.

Customers began to dribble in with friendly greetings. The early breakfast crowd. They all glanced at the strangers, then ignored them. No real interest in people passing through. A tight-knit community, he bet.

Allie's stomach roiled as she scanned the menu. No greens or veggies of any kind. No amazing short-order cook in sight. Eggs with home fries. Eggs with bacon. Eggs with ham. Stacks of toast or flapjacks.

She *had* to eat something. She was starving. It had been a long time since their last meal, but she wondered if she could hold any of this down. Her stomach was trying to tell her not.

But she couldn't afford to listen. When she spied the biscuits with cream gravy, she decided on them without the gravy. Just a teeny bit of butter she could add herself. Better than white-bread toast.

Hale cocked a brow at her, then went to the counter to order. It wasn't long before the food appeared and he carried plates to the table. Napkins poked out at her from a metal dispenser, flanked by salt and pepper shakers and the inevitable squeeze bottle of ketchup. The flatware was already on the table, wrapped in more paper napkins.

"You sure that's enough for you?" he asked.

"I don't feel much like eating." The biscuits aston-ished her, however. Amazingly light, not the hockey pucks she'd anticipated.

Hale had his usual large portion. The guy must have a cast-iron stomach. The way he'd been eating on the trip, he must be getting close to a heart attack despite working out and staying in such good shape.

When they finished, Hale paid the bill and they headed out to the car again.

"Funny," Allie said. "I used to dream of seeing this much snow. Now I'm getting sick of it."

"Want your palm trees and jacarandas, huh?"

"Something warm. That's all." Something other than white and dark green and occasional neon signs. This road stop hadn't even bothered with a weary string of Christmas lights.

Soon they'd find another fleabag and spend the day there, evidently. Changing patterns. She wondered if it worked.

Miles later Hale surprised her by pulling into the parking lot of a grocery in a tiny town. "I'll be right back," he said.

Allie should have wanted to go inside for the change of scenery, but something had made her listless, as much as it had killed her appetite. Some part of her must have settled into a cocoon of self-protection. How else was she supposed to deal with this?

Hale returned about fifteen minutes later with a cou-ple of plastic bags. "A cornucopia," he said as he put the bags behind the front seat.

"Of what?"

"We'll be stopping for the day soon. You'll see."

The next fleabag motel looked a lot more reputable than the last one. But maybe her measuring stick had gone nuts, too.

She said nothing to Hale as he carried everything inside.

"New clothes next stop," he said as he placed the plastic bags beside her.

"Sounds good. These are getting overworn."

"I haven't seen a place," he answered.

"Me neither."

Scintillating conversation.

He spoke again as he pulled his jacket off. "Don't want to peek in those bags?"

She looked at them. "Should I?"

"I think so."

When she opened them, she gasped. A pint of fresh strawberries and large bag of seedless grapes. Containers of fruit yogurt. Bananas. Hummus and pita chips.

"I never expected such a good selection, not there," he remarked. "Anyway, there are plastic utensils at the bottom of the bags. Help yourself."

She raised her gaze. "But why?"

"Because I've fed you enough junk food for a lifetime. So save your arteries and dig in."

The gesture nearly brought tears to her eyes. Such a caring, observant thing to do.

He'd also bought some small paper plates, and she had no trouble loading one. Strawberries and grapes first. Then some yogurt. Oh, Lord, it was heaven.

"Aren't you going to eat?" she asked him before popping a delicious strawberry into her mouth.

"In a few. I want to see you fill up first. I'm going to watch you." He waggled his eyebrows at her. "No picking."

"I couldn't pick at any of this." She smiled. "How did you know?"

"Could be a breakfast consisting only of biscuits without gravy. Or it could be that I don't eat diner food all the time, either. Should have occurred to me sooner."

"You didn't want to stop long most places."

"I wasn't long."

No, he hadn't been, and the yogurt tasted like ambrosia. As did all the fresh fruit. "Please eat," she said as she opened her second yogurt. She had begun to feel full. "I'm almost out of room."

"I suggest the hummus and chips when we wake up later."

"Good idea."

When she finished gorging, feeling contentedly replete for the first time in a while, she lay back on the single bed, fully clothed, and spread her arms. "I'm going into a food coma."

"Go ahead. Enjoy it."

It really wasn't long before she fell into dreams. These were happier dreams than any she'd had since the start of this trek.

HALE WATCHED HER sleep for a while, thinking she looked like an angel, then grabbed another purchase out of the bottom of one of the bags.

An hour later, when he emerged from the bathroom amid steam from his long, hot shower, he was clean-shaven. He always wore a beard, whether short or long, but the times called for looking very different. He supposed Allie would be shocked.

He felt a flicker of amusement over her imagined response. Time to stop looking like Jim Bridger.

WHEN ALLIE WOKE, the early winter night had fallen. Then she saw Hale sitting in the chair by the window, reading the atlas in the light of a lamp.

Was that *Hale*? She rubbed her eyes. "Hale, what happened?"

He looked up from the atlas. "Face met razor. Razor won."

My God, he was handsome. She'd guessed it, but now that she could see his square jaw and get a real look at his mouth, she no longer had to imagine.

"Changing your appearance?" she guessed.

"My best friend wouldn't recognize me right now. Beards are a great way to change your appearance but removing one can have the same effect after a period of time. Are you shocked?"

"I kinda like the way you look now."

He returned to his atlas without replying. Either he didn't care what she thought, which was highly likely, or after his burst of caring last night he was returning to his monolith persona.

She rose, feeling grimy after sleeping in her clothes. "How long before we have to go?"

"Long enough for you to take a shower if you want."

She took him up on it and returned wearing her last fresh change of clothes. She felt remarkably better.

Then even better when she saw he'd broken out the hummus and the pita chips. Plastic knives decorated the paper plates.

"Eat a little," he suggested. "It's going to be a long night."

She didn't doubt it. When Hale got behind the wheel, there was almost no stopping him. He still occupied the lone chair, so she perched on the foot of the bed facing him. He pulled the small table over between them with its passengers of plates and food.

"There's still a bit of fruit left if you want it, and a banana or two."

She smiled, putting some chips and hummus on her plate. "Unless you want them, I'll save them for later."

She was still getting used to his new look. The absence of a beard made him so attractive. Not "pretty" attractive. Not the look of some Hollywood heartthrob, but attractive in a harder way.

And he still struck her as dangerous. Which he probably was, but she hoped never to see that side of him. She hoped they got through this somehow without violence, but the way he'd spoken a few times warned her that it was not going to be that easy, especially from the men who were following them.

It wasn't long before they were on the road again, sunshine bright from a blue sky, sparkling off the snow that seemed to be growing deeper on either side of the road. She was grateful for the darkly tinted windows or she would have been wishing for sunglasses.

"Put your hat on," Hale said in the late afternoon.

"Why?"

"Shopping for clothes, remember?"

They were driving along what seemed to be the main street of a quaint town with strong hints of its Western and Edwardian past. Called Conard City according to the green-and-white sign at the city limits. Grandiose name for such a small place.

"Charming," Allie murmured as she drank in the Christmas lights hanging from lampposts. The decorated tree in a central square. This place had spared nothing in the way of holiday ornamentation, including the businesses and houses she could see. It was beautiful and magnetic with its bright joy in the season.

Hale pulled over, parking near the front of a store labeled *Freitag's Mercantile*. A mercantile? Who used that term anymore?

Age showed in the darkened green wood that was highlighted by a dark-hued reddish color. A little gold paint here and there.

"Let's go in," Hale said as he switched off the ignition. "We need warmer jackets as well as everything else. Just remember—"

She cut him off. "I know. Don't buy anything I actually like."

"Except possibly candy."

Candy? Where had that come from? But her legs were thrilled to be out of the car and walking again. She still didn't feel stretched out by the time they walked through the big door with paned windows.

Inside quite a few people were wandering around

with the small carts that clothing stores often had. They appeared to be shopping for gifts and were all smiling and looking quite happy.

Allie envied them. Then, with a quiet sigh, she started looking through stacks of folded clothes and putting them in the small cart that Hale pushed for her.

More dull colors when she was more than ready for something brighter. She pulled out a red sweatshirt and, when she heard no critical commentary, she took the matching pants, as well.

Then, to please him, she turned to navy blue.

There was a green sweater she couldn't resist, and its pattern had rows of polar bears and penguins. Ha! When he wasn't looking, she tucked in a pair of seasonal pajamas. Maybe she'd get away with it.

Again no critical commentary. All Hale said was, "Don't forget a warmer jacket."

So along with a couple of pairs of jeans and two flannel shirts, she chose a loden-green jacket that wouldn't go with her sweat suits unless she wanted to look like an ornament herself. What was so bad about that?

More undies, of course. Socks, a couple of bras. Mittens. Basics.

But then Hale drew her over to some boots with high tops.

"The ones with the wool liners are best," he said, "but your choice."

Now she became practical. Meanwhile, as they'd strode the aisles, he'd outfitted himself. Nothing that would stand out, of course, but to her an interesting choice was a white parka and snow pants. Neither the pants nor jacket made a sound when he rubbed the fabric together. The kind of thing a hunter might want.

Her heart nearly stopped. Camouflage for this weather? With a hand that nearly shook, she pointed. "Should I get white, too?"

He shook his head. "You won't have a need if I have anything to say about it."

So he was planning again. Far from comforting her, it made her more nervous. A lot more nervous. Especially when he picked out a white balaclava.

Oh, man. Ready for winter warfare?

When they were back in the car, piles of handled paper bags behind them, she asked, "Have you learned something?"

"Not yet."

To her surprise, he didn't head out of town, but instead drove west to another one of those motels, right across from a grumbling truck stop. With a diner, of course.

Night had fallen by the time he checked them in and started replacing older clothes with the new ones.

"Hale?" she asked.

"Yeah?"

"I want to go for a walk. I'd like to see some of the decorations." She knew she was pushing him, but she didn't care. This issue was never going to get resolved if they kept moving.

He looked up. "Wait until I can go with you."

Wow. She went to the bathroom and began to change into her red sweat suit, her new boots. Then she went looking for her jacket, sort of puffy enough to be a green Michelin man. She giggled when she saw herself in the mirror.

"Not used to it?" he asked mildly.

"How would I be? I look funny."

She saw him almost smile. "You'll look like most everyone around here right now."

He was ready about twenty minutes later, wearing his new white jacket. "Let's go and see your Christmas lights."

The boots felt odd on her feet, with thick soles and the wool liners, but she adjusted fast enough and he was right about the warmth.

"Why the liners?" she asked as he locked the door behind them. A new blue watch cap pretty much covered her hair.

"So that if you get snow inside your boot, the wool will keep your feet warm. Then the liner can be pulled out and dried reasonably quickly."

"Good idea."

As they walked toward town, he astonished her by taking her hand.

"Hale?"

"We're a couple," he said quietly. "We should look like one."

Oh. A ruse. She only wished it made her feel more comfortable rather than as if an electric tingle ran up her arm.

The closer they drew to the town center, the brighter and more frequent the holiday lights became. Storefronts were decorated with lighted wreaths. Strands of multicolor light swags hung from their fronts. Even the sheriff's office was decked out.

"Oh," she breathed, "this place looks like a Christmas card."

"It sure does."

Then she remembered what he'd told her about Christmas. "I'm sorry. If you want to go back to the motel…"

"I'm fine. Enjoy yourself."

She looked at him, and while his expression was grave, he didn't look as if he were miserable. Although how one could tell with him, she couldn't imagine.

But she took him at his word as they walked along sidewalks dusted with salt and heard the faint strands of Christmas carols drifting from some businesses and houses.

She paused at the city square and exclaimed with delight, "Oh, look, they're having Christmas carols here at night. But not tonight," she added in disappointment.

"Tomorrow night," he said.

He'd move them on before then. She refused to give in to her disappointment, though. He was letting her take this walk through a town that wore a snowy cloak of Christmas.

But, man, she was getting ready to raise a ruckus about this, and Christmas could give her an excuse.

HALE REMAINED ON alert but he was surprised by the number of people who offered holiday greetings as they passed. Smiling faces.

Who had made this damn town so friendly?

If anyone felt disturbed by the strangers in their midst, they gave no evidence of it. Bustling along with shopping bags and bright smiles on cold-reddened cheeks, they seemed to be anticipating a wonderful event. A happy one.

He imagined excited children counting the days in their homes. Parents trying to sneak parcels and bags past them. Stockings hanging ready and waiting.

The kind of Christmas he'd never known.

They turned a corner and soon came upon a storefront labeled "Conard City Bakery." Mouthwatering smells emanated from it and Hale looked at Allie's delighted face. "Want to go in?"

"Absolutely."

Tonight all restrictions were off. The reality of morning would hit soon enough.

Inside a pretty middle-aged woman greeted them. Tables dotted the floor in front of a display case. Tables covered with real white tablecloths.

"We're not usually open at this time of day," she told them with a smile. "But at this time of year, who could pass up fresh Christmas cookies and hot chocolate?"

Allie looked up at him and he answered her silent plea. "Not us," he said. He looked around the dining area and saw only a few people.

"I'm Melinda," the woman said.

"Alice and Hank," Hale answered. "Nice to meet you."

"Just take a look at the case and decide what kind of cookies you'd like. And we have tea and coffee as well as hot chocolate."

Apart from frosted and sprinkled sugar cookies, there were gingerbread men, pfeffernusse cookies the like of which he hadn't seen since Germany. He chose a few of them himself.

Allie was in a "one of each" mood and soon had a ceramic plate full of them.

"Enjoy," Melinda said. "I have doggie bags if you take more than you want right now."

The hot chocolate was creamy and thick, and as he watched Allie's happy expression, he was moved to share a memory.

"I saw a lot of places like this when I was in Germany."

She looked up from her chocolate. "Like this?"

"Exactly like this. A bakery, with tables and chairs. Seemed like there was one on every street. All I know is that when you wanted to sit down and enjoy a bowl of soup or a hot beverage, they had them. And if you took a table, they never, ever rushed you along. You could stay for hours if you wanted."

"That would be nice."

"It sure was. And some of them had rooms set aside for meetings of various kinds. All welcoming and friendly."

"It sounds so gracious." Her smile had widened.

"Yup. In fact, most of the people I met were gracious. One of the things I liked was that well-behaved dogs were allowed everywhere. A place we stopped for lunch there was a man with a very small dog at the next table over. Naturally, his dog wanted to investigate me."

"Of course." She laughed.

"So the little bugger came over and I reached down to pet him. Which caused the man at the next table to engage in conversation. He was German but with a great command of English. And he was full of jokes. I laughed a lot."

She tried to imagine him laughing, especially a lot. She couldn't quite do it. "It sounds like a great experience."

"It was," he agreed. Then he fell silent again. He'd made his attempt at conversation and it had worked to judge by her expressions and her laugh. Now he was out of words.

"Now I want to go to Germany, too," she remarked.

"Too?"

"Oh, I have a whole list. Scotland. Ireland. France. The list keeps growing. To get a Eurail pass and stay anywhere I want for a few days."

"You will."

Her smile became crooked. "If I survive this."

He had no reply for that. He couldn't be 100 percent certain he'd save her. No one could. Certainly not with a surreptitious hit man on their heels.

Which turned his thoughts in exactly the wrong direction during this brief time when Allie looked happier than she had since the outset of this flight. He felt his face turn expressionless again, the best thing under the circumstances. Since Allie, he'd begun to wonder if he was an open book.

He was definitely talking more than was his custom.

After their relaxed dessert, they walked around a bit more while Allie drank in the sights. The streets had virtually emptied, the people evidently gone to their homes.

Then back to the motel. By this time the diner across the highway had turned on some colorful lights. Even some of the rumbling trucks were lit up with red and green, and others had wreaths over their front grilles.

Everyone was participating.

"Want a meal?" he asked Allie. "Cookies didn't count."

"Calorie-wise they sure did."

He shook his head slightly. She must have seen it.

"But of course," she said, "you must need more than a couple of cookies. Let's go."

He hoped she'd eat something more substantial. He knew three cookies wouldn't be enough for him.

The diner had been bitten by the Christmas bug. Inside carols played, and tables were covered with plastic cloths that had been decorated with poinsettias.

There were more poinsettias on the end of the counter, and a lighted and decorated artificial tree in one corner.

He sighed inwardly. "The First Noel" and "Silent Night" didn't make him a happy camper, although over the years he'd become more immune.

Allie darted a look his way, as if she realized this might be uncomfortable for him. Damn him for ever telling her that story. He refused to let his face twitch a single muscle, even when they studied menus. *Just focus on eating.*

He ordered his goodly portion, this time a burger and fries. He was relieved when Allie discovered enough appetite to ask for a side of breakfast sausage and an

English muffin. He was sure, calories notwithstanding, that a few cookies wouldn't get her through the night. Nor would she probably want the selection in her doggie bag later.

They should be on the road already, but he was willing to give her another day. He hadn't heard anything yet to make him wonder if danger could arrive that fast and she clearly needed the break. Hell, he did, too.

She skipped her usual shower. The room was still so chilly, and no matter how much he looked, he couldn't find a thermostat.

Energy savings, he supposed. And maybe this temperature didn't feel all that cold to people who were used to winter.

Whatever, she was in the bathroom just long enough to change into her new set of flannel pajamas. Then, with nothing but a "Good night," she disappeared under the covers.

Which left him to spend the night thinking about the difficulties ahead. He had to find a way to end this soon.

What he didn't expect was the difficulty morning would bring.

Chapter Ten

Allie had finished dressing, including her parka, cap, mittens and boots. He was almost there himself.

Then she dropped her bomb. "I'm not leaving."

Here we go, he thought. He'd expected her stubbornness to make serious trouble sooner or later. The moment had arrived.

He summoned his most reasonable tone. "Allie, we've got to go. Until I can get those guys in my sights, it's not safe."

"I don't care." Her chin thrust forward, a belligerent expression he liked but would never admit.

"I'm serious," he started. "Your life—"

"I don't have a life anymore. You're not stealing Christmas from me, too."

Stealing Christmas? He didn't want to be compared to the Grinch. Or Ebenezer Scrooge. "Ellis is trying to take your life," he pointed out.

"Well, I'm paying you to protect me. So protect me! If we never stop running, you'll never catch them."

Hale felt as if his head would explode with frustration. She was out the door before he could stop her. He finished tying his final boot and grabbed his jacket as quickly as he could to chase after her, catching her before she quite passed the motel.

"I *am* protecting you."

"From what? All the pleasure and happiness in life? What's the point?"

"Allie…"

"Don't *Allie* me. You know it's true. Just because you're so miserable doesn't mean *I* have to be."

Ouch. "Let's go discuss this over breakfast."

"Discuss what? I'm not going anywhere! Besides, I've had it with diners."

"I'm not fond of them myself, truth be told. I saw a café in town. Let's go there."

"It's probably the same. Do people in this part of the country eat anything else?"

"That's not fair," he pointed out calmly. "Let's try the café. It's probably not very busy at this hour."

She stopped walking and faced him. "You're not talking me out of this. Damn it, Hale, you work for *me*. I am sick to death of being dragged around like luggage."

He didn't bother reminding her what his real job was, what she'd hired him to do. Nope, she wouldn't stand for that right now.

When she agreed to the café, he steeled himself for a sea of Christmas music and red-and-green decorations. Probably even a tree. God, this town was taking the season way over the top.

He was right about one thing, however. It was only moderately busy this morning and they were able to get a table away from the windows. He hated windows. Too exposed.

At least the menu wasn't decorated around the edges with poinsettia leaves or little Christmas balls or bells. No decorated tablecloths, just bare plastic tops. And the menu varied from the places they'd been eating.

Despite her mood, Allie didn't resist him over breakfast. She chose a bowl of mixed fruit, which proved to be large enough to assure him she was actually eating. Plenty of coffee, too.

Some knot of worry that had begun to tighten inside him let go. They'd deal with the rest of it later. They *had* to.

For now, she'd have her day. *One* day.

"This is good canned fruit," she remarked. "No sweetened syrup."

Okay, she was unquestionably eating. He relaxed a hair more and ate almost as if he were at a training table. Which he very nearly was. They both worked out in the evenings, but his exercising was far more strenuous. It had to be. He had no idea of the problems he might face and where they might come from.

To borrow the Coast Guard motto: *Semper Paratus.* Always prepared. He tried to be.

After breakfast, served by a surly waitress named Mavis, Allie started her walk around the town. Joy. Not.

But for her it seemed to be. Smiles kept dancing over her face, and she greeted people as they passed by, many of them loaded down with bags.

"Why don't people shop earlier?" he asked.

"I don't know. I always meant to, then faced the last

minute. And too often some special item I picked for someone had vanished. You'd think I'd have learned."

Well, that was another grin he couldn't quite hide.

They paused at the courthouse square, with its requisite soldier statue on a podium, and Allie clapped her mittened hands together. "Oh, look! There are packages under the tree now."

Yes, there were. Okay, way over the top. Worse, having her in the open like this was winding him up tight.

She asked, "Why don't they get wet?"

Two couples, hearing her, came over. They looked like a pair of grandparents and their adult children.

"They're just wrapped for looks," the younger woman explained. "Hi, I'm Josie." She introduced the other three as Mary, Jacob and Wesley.

"I'm Alice. And this is my fiancé. I won't give him a name."

A sideways swipe, Hale decided.

The three others laughed.

"The presents are a clever idea," Allie said, pointing to the tree. "So festive."

"It's a placeholder," Wesley said.

Allie's brow knit. "For what?"

"Real presents," Mary chimed in. "On Christmas Eve, around noon, we bring out all the wrapped toys that people have donated."

"For kids who might not have anything under the tree at all," Wesley, the older man, explained. "We've got a tree in the courthouse lobby, and all the names and ages are on paper circles dangling from it. You pick one or two and fulfill the wishes. Sometimes it's so sad, though."

Josie nodded. "It brings you to tears when a four-year-old's Christmas wish is for a new winter jacket."

"Or mittens," Jacob said. "Or shoes or boots. They should be wishing for toys."

"Where I used to live," Allie said, "we had the same thing. It was called the Angel Tree."

"We ought to do that," Mary said, looking at the others.

"How late can you donate gifts?" Allie asked.

Hale smelled a shopping expedition coming.

"Well, right up until the party," Josie answered. "But the closer it gets to Christmas, the more we hope folks will wrap them before they bring them. Oh, and please don't forget to put the little name tags on them." She laughed.

Allie looked at Hale. "I'd like to go in and see the tree."

"I was sure you would," he answered, hoping he sounded more like a loving mate than a tooth-grinding bodyguard.

They said farewell to the nice people and Allie headed straight for the courthouse. At least the steps were salted, he thought irritably. His job didn't involve taking her to the ER with a cracked skull because she fell.

Bah, humbug, he thought, then stopped himself. *No Ebenezer Scrooge. Just try to enjoy Allie's enjoyment.* That was better than fury over her stubbornness.

At the tree inside, they met more smiling people—

God, did everyone in this town perpetually smile?—and waited patiently while Allie examined green-and-red balls cut out of construction paper. Finally she had six of them and she turned to the other people checking out the tree.

She asked, "Where is the best place to go shopping for the kids?"

"Freitag's Mercantile," two of them answered at once. They laughed.

"Yeah," one of them said. "They're stocked up for kids this time of year and you can find anything. Not all of it is expensive."

Which might well be a consideration for that group, he thought. None of them looked as if they'd bought new jackets or hats in a while.

They were generous anyway. His crabby mood lightened a bit. Some people, he reminded himself, could be truly good.

Allie beelined straight for the Mercantile. Apparently she remembered its location, not that it would have been hard to miss. She paused frequently, however, to drink in one house or another.

He remarked, "They sure go all-out around here." Couldn't she just keep moving?

"I think it's beautiful."

It wasn't just lights strung from eaves and perhaps over shrubs or a fir tree. Nope. Glowing snowmen. Bursts of small lights that looked almost like sparklers along the sidewalks. Santa in his sleigh with reindeer. A yard full of lighted polar bears. And it seemed to him that some of the decorations had been collected over the years. Their ages showed a bit.

Impressive, he admitted. These folks were determined to enjoy this season. As Allie was.

Just until tomorrow.

She certainly had fun picking out gifts at Freitag's. She studied her handful of paper Christmas baubles, then began choosing items. One thing she added, however, were six teddy bears in green costumes and red Santa hats. That surprised him.

"Six?" he asked. "Did some kid want six teddy bears?"

"No, but every child should get a little something special, a gift they didn't even ask for."

Well, that was something else. Then he remembered she'd mentioned it once before.

She also bought a bunch of large gift bags. By the time they departed the store, he'd used quite a wad of her money from his wallet and was loaded down like a pack mule. They headed back to the motel.

Which he honestly didn't mind. It would get her off the street. But Allie was having fun, and somehow the fun was rubbing off on him. Just a bit, he assured himself. But damn, he kept getting these stupid half smiles on his face.

In their room, the booty came out. Space rockets, boxes of LEGO, baby dolls, a pink winter parka that looked impossibly small to his eyes. And into each extra-large bag went not only a teddy bear but also a small, warm blanket he hadn't noticed her buying.

"I'm impressed," he told Allie.

"It's not much."

"That isn't what I meant."

Their eyes met, then she flushed and turned quickly away. "I wanted small candy canes to put in these, but I wasn't sure if I should. What if one of these children has tooth problems?"

"I never would have thought of that. Good on you."

"I don't usually think in those terms," she said, her voice thickening a little. "I mean, I always buy a gift or two for the Angel Tree at home, but I've never had to be in a position where I considered such things. I've been so lucky!"

Until now, he thought. "Are you cold yet?"

"Well, I warmed up in here. But I want to go to the bakery for some hot soup and chocolate."

Out into the danger zone again. God, he hoped she wasn't determined to turn herself into bait before he'd winnowed the pursuers enough.

"There's Christmas caroling in the square tonight," she reminded him as they walked hand in hand toward the bakery.

Of course there was. He sighed, trying not to think about how every minute was increasing the threat level.

ALLIE HEARD THE sigh and wondered if she'd brought back bad memories for him. She'd promised herself she wouldn't do that, but she suspected she had anyway with her insistence on having a bit of Christmas. Still, she was determined.

"I'm sorry," she said. "I guess I've made you miserable."

"No," he answered.

"Are you sure?"

"Well, I'm not in a Scrooge mood."

That brought a laugh out of her. "You can be nice sometimes, Hale."

He didn't reply and she let it go. She'd probably gotten more words out of him in the last two days than he ordinarily spoke in two years. Or so that had been her initial impression.

He probably hated having her out in the open like this, she realized. He'd been doing his best to keep her out of sight except for brief periods.

He hadn't objected, though. Maybe he felt the threat was far enough away for now. Although how he was ever going to catch the bad guys she couldn't imagine. Keeping her away from them didn't allow Hale to get very far from her.

But he seemed confident enough so he must have a plan or be constructing one.

Besides, Max wouldn't have recommended him if he didn't completely trust Hale.

"I miss Max," she announced as they sat at a table with potato soup and their cocoa. "We always spend a lot of time together at the holidays. Max loves them."

Hale nodded. "Does he? I wouldn't know. I'm usually working."

She wondered if that was true or just an excuse to stay away from Max's cheer. "I love his hot cider, and sometimes he makes a fabulous Irish coffee. My friends were spending their time with family on Christmas Eve, but Max always invited a few of his friends from the cop shop. Those guys could really get a party going."

"I don't doubt it. Even in Afghanistan Christmas managed to arrive. Even at the distant forward bases where I was stationed. Invariably someone would pull in some bedraggled plant as a stand-in for a Christmas tree. One time someone cadged some foil and the guys crushed it into balls to make ornaments."

Allie put her chin in her hand and listened, delighting in imagining it.

"Then one year we were able to light one of those silly trees. John Hansford's wife sent him a string of battery-operated lights. Pretty enough, changing through a series of colors. Unfortunately, Hansford's wife didn't send a hundred batteries along with it. We all laughed ourselves sick when we discovered the strand would only operate for about three hours before draining the batteries."

A faint smile played around his mouth, and Allie drank it in. It seemed Christmas hadn't *always* been a bad time for him. Then she watched him shut down again, as if he believed he had said too much.

She felt him pushing constantly against the atmosphere in this town. He didn't want to let it in.

Well, too bad. She wasn't going anywhere. This had to be settled. Even if he exploded.

As the light faded from the sky, a whole new layer appeared. Decorations that hadn't been lit all day sprang to life. More people arrived on the streets carrying bags and boxes. The Mercantile appeared to have a line waiting out front. The bakery had placed some plastic chairs and tables on the sidewalk to handle the overflow.

And Allie was indefatigable in her desire to drink it all in. They'd been outdoors most of the day.

He didn't mind that as a rule. He'd spent years outdoors in less hospitable places. But having Allie out in the crowds stretched his nerves.

But she was having a good time. Everywhere she went, she fell into conversation with people. In no time at all she'd be in the midst of a group of locals laughing along with them.

She had a gift for being the welcome stranger in this place.

He must have seemed like a dour lug standing beside her.

Which was fine by him. He *hated* casual conversation.

Anyway, he stood there holding four of the six bags she had filled, and getting to those courthouse steps might take a long time, given how she kept stopping to talk.

Nor was he going to offer to take the bags inside without her. No way was he going to leave her alone. So he stood there, manufacturing some semblance of a smile while she made friends she wasn't going to see again after tonight.

Then she saw that a crowd was gathering in the middle of the square. "Ooh," she said. "Almost time for caroling. Let's get these bags inside now."

Standing there with those colorful, large bags was making him feel like a Christmas tree himself. He'd be glad to dump them. In the lobby, another group of smiling people were gathering the gifts on a large red tarp. More conversation. At this point Hale would have been glad to see one furious face.

But he never stopped scanning all those cheerful faces, looking for anything that didn't strike him right. Anything, however small. Time to check in with Stu again, he decided. He needed to know where the hunters were now.

But for the moment all he could do was watch and wait.

And endure the carols. Even in his miserable childhood, he hadn't escaped Christmas music. Anytime he went to the stores, he was drenched in it. For some it brought back happy feelings. For him it was just a reminder of bad times.

Allie got into it, though. The group in the center of the square seemed to be a more practiced choir, but they weren't there to sing alone. No, everybody surrounding the square joined in. The rising voices, some clearly out of tune, filled the area with a haunting beauty.

He quit trying to fight it. Would it kill him for just one evening to quit nursing old pains and grudges? He believed they drove him, made him the man he had become, a man who'd improved himself. But he didn't need the memories just then.

Allie, beside him, sang in a beautiful flute-like soprano. Right on key, too. He watched her face between glances around them, so bright and shiny, and hoped she'd never lose that expression.

He was damn well going to do his best to prevent it.

DESPITE LONGING TO share the holidays with her friends, Allie was having a wondrous time. That Christmas postcard she'd always eyed with envy surrounded her now, absorbing her, filling her with the very magic she'd always imagined.

Deep within she knew this was a special moment in time, that soon enough these people would leave behind the beauty for the drudgery of everyday life. But she refused to think of that. Right now the world was full of beautiful music and, when snow began to fall gently, the night couldn't have been any more perfect.

A little over an hour later, the concert ended and people began to drift apart. That somehow seemed perfect, too. Trailing away to warm homes with Christmas trees and maybe excited children.

Several people invited her to their homes for hot cider and cookies, but a glance at Hale's face told her she'd better not. He'd reached his limit with this stuff.

A twinge of guilt struck her and she declined the invitations pleasantly, explaining that she was growing tired after a busy day.

"Maybe tomorrow, then," man replied.

"Maybe," she answered.

As they walked back to the motel, Hale said two things. "We need some hot food. And we're leaving in the morning."

Allie gritted her teeth. She'd found wonder and magic and he had no good reason to tear her away. Unless he could give her a reason other than that they needed to keep moving. But moving meant he'd never be able to face the threat.

She left that conversation for later, deciding he was right about getting a meal.

The City Café had a line out front, so he said they were going to the truck stop. Okay, then. As long as it was hot and filling.

The truck stop was busy but still had plenty of tables. Allie noticed that Hale steered her away from the windows to a table in the corner. He sat facing outward, scanning the room.

"Do you ever relax?" she asked.

"Not on a job."

That's right, she thought as she ordered up oatmeal, scrambled eggs and coffee. She was just a job to him. Maybe she ought to be grateful he'd given her this one day. Except he hadn't given it to her. She'd taken it for herself.

And she was not leaving unless he had a damn good reason for insisting.

"I wish I could call my friends," she said wistfully. Her thoughts of them were growing ever stronger, especially during this season. "I'm seriously homesick."

"Homesick?"

"Yeah. My stomach feels hollow. I'm missing home. That's not unnatural, but I just can't keep this up forever."

"I'm not planning on that."

She frowned as she finished her oatmeal. "Just how are you going to do that when you won't let these guys get close?"

"I'm working on it."

The wall clamped into place again. She sighed. Every

so often he'd peek out from behind it, but only in little bits. Somewhere inside him was undoubtedly a fascinating man, but she'd never know. Not when he kept his guard so high.

Just then a tall man with a burn-scarred cheek limped in. Wearing a brown insulated jacket over a dark brown uniform, he didn't need the badge on his chest to shout *police*. Instead of heading to the counter or a table, he came straight toward them.

"Howdy," he said and pulled a chair over. "I'm Sheriff Gage Dalton. Welcome to our little part of the world."

Allie smiled. "My dad was a cop."

Dalton gave her a crooked smile in return. "Family, then."

Allie was about to reply when Hale took over. "People worried about us?"

"Not much, but strangers around here tend to stand out. You a vet?"

Hale nodded. "Marines."

"You have that cut to your jib. So what brings you our way? We're not exactly on the tourist trail."

This time Allie tensed a bit. Did people think they were dangerous? She hadn't gotten that feeling from anyone so far.

Hale answered. "We're on a long road trip. The state highway led us here and Alice couldn't resist staying. All this Christmas caught her attention."

Dalton smiled crookedly again, as if the burn scar tugged at his mouth. "It'll do that. Still to come, a Christmas parade with Santa, and some reindeer. More caroling. The gift-giving party on Christmas Eve. Oh, and the Mercantile with bare shelves. If you want anything, better buy it quick."

Allie laughed. "Did you miss anything on your list?"

"I did," he said with a nod. "A group of students will wander around the neighborhoods singing carols, too."

Allie's expression became wistful again. "That must be beautiful."

"Very," the sheriff answered. When a waiter came over, he ordered coffee and a serving of mincemeat pie. Then his attention squared on Hale. "You haven't looked very happy today."

So people had been paying attention to them, eyeing them suspiciously even while being friendly. She looked at Hale, sensing the tension in him.

Hale answered the implied question. "Alice will tell you that I'm the original Grinch. Not my thing."

"It isn't for everyone." Dalton thanked the waiter as he placed a cup of coffee and a slice of pie in front of him. "I enjoy watching so many people get into the spirit around here. Like folks everywhere, we have our squabbles and a few feuds. For a while they get forgotten."

"Must make your job easier," Hale answered.

"Hell, yeah. We'll have a few burglaries as people stuff gifts under their trees, but not many. And we probably won't have to break up any brawls until New Year's Eve." He frowned faintly. "But there are domestics. They seem to rise around this time."

Allie watched Hale's face darken. God, what a subject to come up right now.

But Gage, who was getting through his pie with reasonable speed, remarked, "What do you two do?"

"I'm an accountant," Allie answered. "About as boring as people come."

"Nobody's boring," the sheriff answered. "And you?" he asked Hale.

"Private security."

Dalton's brow lifted. "Mercenary?"

Allie caught her breath.

"Not anymore," Hale answered. "Looked around, didn't like it."

"Good for you." Dalton finished his pie and his coffee. "Well, I won't trouble you folks any longer. Consider this your welcome to Conard County. Nice meeting you."

With a nod, he placed a cowboy hat on his head, one with a sheriff's badge embroidered on the front, then waved as he left.

Only then did Allie notice he was fully armed, even with a collapsible baton. This had been official.

"Wow," she whispered. "Who did we set off?"

"It was probably just a good lawman keeping an eye out. I didn't get the sense that he was suspicious."

"I guess not."

But now more questions roiled in her head. Mercenary? Had he been? What had he done?

WELL, THAT HAD been unfortunate, Hale thought as they finished up their meal and headed back across the highway to their motel. Now Allie had a million questions, their profile had gotten higher, and he might have revealed too much. Hell.

They sure weren't invisible even in a crowd.

The urge to get on the road again was itching at the base of his skull and felt like a cold breath down his spine. Damn it, he needed more info. More idea of where to play this game out while protecting Allie. Whenever possible, he preferred to choose his own ground for the fight. So far he'd been running pretty much blind, knowing only that he had to reduce the number of their followers. He hated it.

He needed to call Stu. Tonight.

When they got back to the room, he suggested that Allie climb into her pajamas and get warm in bed.

"You have to sleep on the floor again tonight," she remarked.

"I've slept in far worse places. At least gravel and stones won't be poking my back."

The joy was gone from her face, he noticed. The conversation with the sheriff had bothered her. Well, it had bothered him, too. Quite a welcoming committee. They'd been scoped and now he had to wonder if Dalton would try to check them out somehow. Not that he had much to go on. Except for the stolen plates on Hale's vehicle.

Crap. He needed to change them again soon, but not in this town. Not if Dalton might run plates.

If he did, Hale and Allie were going to hit the road before Allie's head could spin. Bait? She wanted to be bait? He hadn't missed the suggestion in all her comments about letting those goons get closer. Maybe they ought to leave right now.

He stepped out into the night's deepening cold and pulled out one of his phones. Stu answered on the second ring.

All Hale said was, "Well?"

"The dolls have been sold again. Headed back north a bit and now east."

Hale's jaw clenched so tight that his muscles hurt. "What does that tell you?"

"Me? Only that someone said the word *Badlands*."

Stu had said it. Jokingly. Why would he mention it to any of the other guys? But Stu also knew he couldn't push Hale in any particular direction, that Hale was in charge of this little journey. Had he mentioned it not so jokingly to someone else on their team?

"What does that tell you?" Hale asked.

"Not enough yet. I'm seriously thinking I need to get rid of an armadillo. Damn thing is building a burrow under my foundation."

"Fill it in with cement," Hale said. "Keeps 'em from digging more. At least there."

"Good idea."

Hale hung up, convinced now that someone in his tight little group had sold out. Was passing along information in more than one direction. Ellis could sure offer some huge enticements.

On the other hand, his contacts were an ad hoc group, some guys he'd known in the past who occasionally offered their expertise in one area or another. They should be invisible to outsiders.

Should have been, he corrected himself. Unless the traitor had gone looking for an inducement.

He tore the battery out of the phone, along with the SIM, then crossed the highway once more to throw the SIM on one truck and the phone on another. He wasn't ready for the battle yet, not in this town, all involved in seasonal joy.

When he returned to the relative warmth of the motel room, he smelled a recent shower and shampoo. Allie was cuddled up under blankets, sitting up and waiting for him. Damn it would have been nice if she'd been asleep, her questions waiting while he thought through all this mess.

He sat on the chair, pulling off his jacket and balaclava, unlacing his boots.

"Learn anything?" she asked.

"Yeah. I'm not ready to discuss it." It would only scare her more to learn that he thought there was a traitor. As bad as when he might have to tell her that a hired hit man was on her trail.

He had to restrain himself from throwing a boot in rage. This situation was bad enough without a mole in his midst. He changed to fresh woolly socks and began to make himself a pallet on the floor.

"Hale?"

"Yeah?"

"There's room on this bed if you're tired of playing martyr."

He stopped breathing. What was she suggesting?

"I'm not making a move on you," she said forthrightly. "Just that I hate seeing you sleep on the floor all the time. You can sleep on top of the covers."

He started breathing again. Allie was truly desirable, but not now. He couldn't afford anything that might throw his emotions into high gear. He had to stay clear-headed.

"I'll think about it," he replied. "Thanks."

"Your choice. And I'll save my questions for later. You look like you have enough on your plate."

God, was he becoming transparent?

"It's okay," he said as reassuringly as he could. "I just need to figure out some things."

Well, he told himself, if there was a mole, maybe he could use him. All he had to do was decide how.

Chapter Eleven

As if Hale didn't already have an overloaded plate, Allie dumped more onto it in the morning. He said, "Time to get on the road."

"I'm not leaving."

Here we go again. "Oh, hell. We're sticking out like sore thumbs in this town."

"Well, you didn't want to go to ground in a big city. I like it here. I like Christmas. I like the way these people are doing it. Besides, you can't get near these guys if they can't get near me. I am *not* going."

She had a point, wrong-headed though it might be. He said nothing as he pulled on his boots. Thinking about it, he decided that at this point he just needed to stay on high alert. Maybe until Christmas was over. He could do that, surely. Besides, if he just grabbed her and threw her in the car, it would be kidnapping, job or not.

And the enemy was headed in the wrong direction, at least now.

For now.

He needed to figure out how to use this mole to his advantage anyway. He gave up the fight with Allie before it began and prepared himself for another day swamped in heavy-duty cheer.

Treat it like a mission, he told himself. Just another mission. At least the locals wouldn't be lobbing grenades his way.

"Okay," he said.

She froze in the process of reaching for her own boots. "Really? I'm not trying to make you crazy."

"You do that just by breathing. Prepare yourself for another day in the cold, woman. We'll drink in every drop of your Christmas. And your cussed stubbornness."

"Tough," she answered. "Do your job. On *my* terms."

Her Christmas. Not his. Allie felt a twinge of guilt, then stopped herself. She was paying for this gig. She ought to have something to say about it.

Besides, she'd blow a gasket if she didn't get some time out of his vehicle. Feeling confined didn't begin to cover it. She needed to be out and about, talking to someone besides the Great Stone Face, whose favorite word appeared to be *No*.

And rough, tough Mr. Bodyguard could just deal with it.

Anyway, it had come to the point where fleeing seemed like a useless option, whether he thought so or not.

In the daylight, Conard City had lost none of its charm. The light snowfall last night had whitened the town's blanket even more, obscuring any signs of dirt or oil that might have come from traffic.

What was even better for Allie was being greeted by name, by people who stopped, despite the frigid weather, to speak with her a bit about whether she was enjoying herself.

"I'm having a wonderful time," she replied. "This town is beautiful."

Several mentioned a hope that she would stay at least through Christmas. "You don't want to miss the gift giving on Christmas Eve."

"No, I don't," she agreed with a smile. She didn't glance at Hale as she said so, because she imagined he must be looking like a steam engine ready to blow its boiler.

She wasn't stupid. She understood his concerns. Surely a few days couldn't cause a problem. But as far as she'd heard from Mr. Silent, the pursuers hadn't come close. Or not close enough.

Where would they go from here, anyway? He was being silent about that, too. Merely speaking of "plans" said nothing at all.

She decided they should have brunch at the City Café, which she had learned was locally known as Maude's Diner.

"That Maude is something else," a woman named Betty told her. "She's owned that diner at least since I was a kid, and I don't think I've ever seen her crack a smile. Her daughter is every bit as abrupt and rude. They're characters around here, the kind everyone loves. The kind people write stories about."

Allie laughed. "I haven't really had a chance to see."

"Oh, you will," Betty assured her. "Wait until she

or her daughter start slamming the crockery down in front of you. Maude even sometimes tells you what to eat." Then Betty giggled.

"What?" Allie asked.

"Oh, years ago, when I was maybe five or so, everyone in town started laughing behind their hands. The previous sheriff, Nate Tate, decided he wanted to lose a little weight. When he dropped in for his usual coffee, he stopped ordering pie."

"Sensible," Allie agreed, smiling.

"Well, he tried to be. Maude was having none of it. She'd slam a plate of pie in front of him, he'd protest he was dieting and she'd retort 'We can't have you blowing away.'"

Allie laughed outright. "Oh, no."

"Oh, yes. She may be cranky and rude, but Maude, in her own way, looks out for people. Maybe not always the right way, but she does."

Allie was still smiling as they walked toward the diner. "I love it here," she said.

"Right now," Hale answered.

"Right now is all I have, and I love it."

The diner was busier as the breakfast crowd gave way to the lunch crowd. There were still tables and Hale once again chose one in a back corner.

Allie shed her jacket and picked up a menu. Then she asked, "What have you got against windows? I'd prefer to be able to look out."

When he didn't answer, she raised her gaze. The man was turning to stone again.

"Hale?"

He shook his head sharply, just once. Then he leaned toward her, keeping his voice low. "Windows are exposure. You can't have everything you prefer."

Ice trickled down her spine at his words. He'd brought back the reality of this whole damn thing. But she wasn't going to let him ruin this for her. This might be her last experience of a normal world. No, she couldn't let him take that away.

It also gave her an insight into the way this man was thinking. *Had* to think. That brought her another shiver. The things he must have seen, must have experienced. She couldn't conceive of it.

Yet the results were sitting right across the table from her. Apart from his horrifying childhood, there must have been other things in his life to turn him into a man who chose to be a bodyguard. Who chose to risk his life protecting others. Who would go to any lengths to protect her.

God. She looked down at the menu again and tried to concentrate on eating. No food since last night should have made her ravenous, but her appetite slipped away.

"Eat," he said presently. "Find something. It's cold out there and you'll need the energy to keep you warm."

She couldn't argue and she didn't want to grow cold so early that she'd need to head back to the motel. She settled on ham hash with a side of whole wheat toast. And this time she was treated to the slamming of plates and cups in front of them. She nearly giggled. Glancing at Hale, she caught amusement flicker across his face.

"You want a pot of coffee?" the woman asked. Her

name tag said she was Maude, an older version of the woman who'd waited on them before.

"Please," Hale answered.

"Damn straight," the woman nearly growled. "Winter. Folks are always wanting a pot. A body can't keep up."

Nonetheless, five minutes later she returned with an insulated carafe. "Bottomless," she said shortly. Then she stomped away.

"Wow," Allie murmured.

"I guess we've met a character," Hale replied. He picked up the carafe and poured for them both.

"You must hate me," Allie said while they ate.

"I don't hate you."

"Well, you hate Christmas and I'm putting you through this. And I'm arguing with you about moving on."

For a minute or two he didn't answer and just as she had decided that he wouldn't, he spoke.

"I don't hate *Christmas*. It's just that I see all these cheerful smiling faces and I can't help but think it's a kind of brainwashing."

That startled her. "Brainwashing?"

"Sure. Everyone is convinced it's a perfect time of year and that they all feel happy and the world is a wonderful place."

Her heart thudded. "But?"

"You have no idea how many of them will go home to discover nothing is perfect. Or feel let down after all the tinsel and partying are gone. Peace and joy to men of good will lasts about fifteen minutes."

"God, Hale." Sorrow for him blossomed inside her, making her ache until she wanted to weep for him.

"Sorry," he said with a shrug. "I shouldn't rain on your parade. But I've had a very different experience all my life."

"Hale…" She wanted to tell him that they could go right now. Leave all this behind to save him the grief.

He shook his head. "You shouldn't have asked. And I sure as hell shouldn't have answered. Enjoy the illusion, Allie. You're entitled to it."

Well, that hardly made her feel any better. Her appetite was truly dead now.

He looked at her as he pulled out his wallet to go pay the bill. "You really don't want to know me, Allie. You really don't."

But as she rose to leave with him, she was thinking exactly the opposite.

IT WAS A good day to kick his own butt, Hale thought as they began to walk along the street again. He knew how to keep his mouth shut. He didn't know, however, why Allie kept getting him to talk. He was walking proof that he shouldn't open his mouth.

It took a little while for Allie's spirits to rise again and he was relieved to see them return. Damn, he needed to stop hitting her with the hard truths. If she wanted to wear rose-colored glasses, then who was he to crack them? Or worse, rip them from her.

If he were to be honest with himself, he might be the one living in his own private illusion of life, one that wasn't pretty.

Allie, of course, found an organic food store and popped inside. Next thing he knew, he was carrying bags of bananas and grapes and raisins and even avocados and fresh green beans.

"I wish I could cook here," she remarked. "That butternut squash is so tempting."

He suspected a few other items tempted her as well, given how she lingered over them. She moved on, though, and before they departed, she purchased a small kitchen knife and some plastic spoons.

That fruit cost a fortune but, since it had come from so far away, it had to. He figured they were going to dine vegetarian tonight. Or at least she was.

Her pleasure in the day had fully returned and he promised himself he'd keep his lips sealed so as not to disturb her again. He rather liked her naïveté and wanted her to keep as much of it as possible.

On the main street, he looked up and down it again, measuring lines of sight while she conversed with more people. This town seemed to be taking to Allie. Which, he admitted, would be very easy to do.

Down the street was the high steeple of a church. That was the only thing he could see with a height to concern him.

"Allie?"

"Yes?"

"Would you mind wandering down to the church? I bet they have some beautiful decorations."

She appeared surprised but nodded. "I'd really like that, Hale."

Apparently they'd both given up on phony first names. He took her mittened hand in his, as per his desire to appear to be a couple, and they strolled along unhurriedly.

Dang, this town was a bustle of activity, and, of course, it slowed them down, because at least half the people were in the mood for a friendly chat with Allie.

He stood back a little, keeping a phony smile plastered on his face, but his eyes darted everywhere. No relaxation for him. One moment of inattention could be one moment too many.

When they reached the church, he was proved right about decoration. The manger scene out front particularly caught his attention. It was no stylized plaster or plastic model. No, the parties standing around the churchyard were all dressed in poor, ragged clothing. *Real* clothing. Joseph and Mary weren't dressed any better.

The manger was a crudely crafted feeding trough full of hay. A small, ragged burlap blanket awaited the arrival of the child.

"Kind of brings it home," he remarked.

"Yeah, they weren't well-to-do. A good reminder. I don't miss the Magi, either."

"As I recall they didn't arrive for a couple of years."

"That's my recollection."

There wasn't even a fake angel. He was impressed despite himself.

"Let's go inside," he suggested. He wanted to scope out the bell tower.

Pine needle wreaths, decorated with white doves, hung from the carved double doors. Inside, the quiet of an empty church greeted them, along with lingering incense. Votive candles burned near the altar.

Other than the huge cross hanging behind the altar, there was no decoration. One rose window, made of stained glass, gleamed above the cross, but all the other windows were plain glass.

No ostentation here, unless you counted the ornately carved wooden pews.

"This is awesome," Allie breathed.

"Wander around. I'd like to take a look at the bell tower."

As he turned toward the door that should lead to the tower stairs, he saw the choir loft hanging in the rear. All the important parts, he thought. Also an excellent position for a sniper if his quarry were inside the church.

The lock on the door he sought wasn't much of a lock. He twisted it and it fell open. Narrow, steep, spiraling stairs greeted him. No more than one person at a time, he thought. Bell ringers must be in short supply.

About twenty feet above, he reached the platform where the bell ringers must stand. Two holes in the ceiling, both with ropes hanging from them, assured him he was right.

The room was fully closed in, possibly against the elements. But the entire spire wasn't closed in, nor could it be or the bells might as well not have been there.

Climbing more stairs, he reached the bell tower. It gave him a panoramic view of the town below.

He might have admired it, but all he could see was that he'd discovered a good sniper's perch. And looking straight out, he could see more.

The library appeared to have a dome on it. There were two more churches with spires. A few houses towered over the town, bespeaking wealth, at least in the past. He'd have bet they'd been turned into rooming houses.

In fact, from what he'd seen of this town, he had trouble understanding how it survived. The outlying ranches? Maybe.

When he finished making a mental map of the town's layout, he returned to the nave. Allie was waiting in one of the rear pews, looking contemplative.

She turned her head as she heard his steps. "How were the bells?"

"Well, they weren't sporting spiderwebs or birds' nests."

She laughed quietly.

"Let's go and get a hot drink or something, then you can decide what you want to see next."

"Sounds good."

AFTER HOT CHOCOLATE, Allie decided to leave the downtown for a walk through the residential neighborhoods. On Front Street, they discovered the row of gracious old Victorian houses, with their third stories and even in one case a widow's walk.

Here the decorations changed a bit. Instead of lights dripping from every eave, and lit polar bears and snowmen, they saw draped green garlands with red bows.

"I bet," she said, "there was a time when the wealthy and important people lived here."

"Looks like it," he agreed.

"It has a lot of charm. I like the gingerbread. I like the decoration, too. As if the people on this street all agreed to the garlands."

"I like it, too," Hale agreed. "Less effusive."

Allie laughed quietly. "You *would* feel that way."

They walked a little farther in silence, then Allie screwed up her courage to ask, "What was that about being a mercenary?"

Hale was quiet for a while, and as they turned the corner onto a different street, he spoke.

There were almost no people around here, Allie had noticed. Maybe that was why he finally spoke. No eavesdroppers.

"I joined a private security firm after I left the Marines. I thought I'd be protecting *people.* Instead I learned that this company was hiring its troops out to foreign governments. Engaging in their wars. I left."

"Why?"

"I'm not a killer for hire."

His words chilled her. God, what this man had seen! Then she said, "That's when you became a bodyguard?"

"I formed my own company. Protecting *individuals* is a whole different ball of wax."

It certainly was, she thought as they walked along a street where the sidewalks hadn't been worn bare of snow by crowds of people as they had been closer to the town center.

"I bet you left some good pay behind."

"The best," he replied.

This man was admirable, she decided. Truly admirable.

She sighed quietly. Her perspective on life was changing, she realized. Starting with having to run from the threat from her former employer. Continuing with the steps Hale kept taking to keep her concealed. She chafed under his restrictions, but he appeared to know what he was doing.

She just wished she knew more about what was going on. Why he was so alert even here? Had she foiled his plan by insisting they remain for a few days?

In the end he hadn't put up a serious argument, but the more she thought about it, the less she liked being baggage. She wanted to *help*.

Again she sighed. He clearly had no intention of letting her. Just follow his orders. Gah! She hated that part, especially when it made no sense to her.

When they reached Main Street again, they turned and headed back toward the town center.

God, she was thirsty for the company of people. She was used to it. The idea that she would spend so much time in the company of one solitary man would have made her laugh.

But if Hale was right, she'd be living exactly this way until he could take care of the threat against her.

But how could he do that? How could he be sure he could do that?

"Hale?"

"Yeah?"

"How are you going to take care of this threat? You haven't said anything."

His jaw tightened. "I'm going to choose my own ground."

She believed that Hale could be an extremely dangerous man when he needed to be.

She was just glad that he was on her side. But she couldn't resist one last poke of the lion. "I still think you need to bait this trap."

HALE NEARLY GROWLED at her, but he'd shot off his mouth again. Damn, how did this woman keep pulling things out of him?

He wasn't proud of those months he'd spent with that so-called security company. The mud had kept rising until he knew that if he wanted to save what was left of his rotten soul, he had to get out.

He hadn't even given notice. He'd walked in one day and told them he was gone and wouldn't be back. Surprisingly, given that he had a contract with them, they didn't argue.

He supposed they figured they were better off without him, without a man who didn't want to do their kind of work. Well, they were. He'd have found a way to sabotage whatever operation they might send him on. He refused to be used that way.

That job had been his own blind spot. He should have had a clue before he signed on.

But lots of people he'd known in the military had signed with those guys and seemed to be quite happy. Men he'd once been proud to know. Men he wasn't proud to know now.

At least he'd rounded up some good buddies who weren't involved in that crap.

Good buddies except for one, it seemed. Because

how else could anyone think he and Allie had headed for the Badlands?

A simmering anger burned in him. Betrayal was one of the worst crimes.

Chapter Twelve

Allie hadn't liked what Hale had said about brainwashing. She might have chosen a different word.

But that didn't make him wrong. If people just carried the Christmas spirit through the rest of the year, the world would be a much better place.

Still, Hale evinced a very dark view of life. Some of what he'd said had told her why. It was sad.

Then he surprised her by speaking again. His routine silence seemed to be dribbling away.

"What about you, Allie? What has your life been like?"

"Happier by far than yours, it would seem."

"Share. You've dragged plenty out of me."

Dragged? She'd only asked. He hadn't needed to answer. But she responded anyway.

"I've been very lucky. It's boring."

"Losing your father that way couldn't have been boring. Nor losing your mother. At least I think you have."

"Yes. She died about the time I started college. Fell down the stairs."

"I'm sorry."

"No need." She grew silent.

"What made you decide to become an accountant?"

She laughed. "Now, that's a boring choice, right?"

"I didn't say that. I wouldn't say that. I'm just curious."

She thought about it, wondering how she could answer in a way anyone else could understand. "Well, I like numbers."

"Interesting. But there are a lot of fields that use numbers."

"I wanted *real* numbers. No variation, no range, none of that. Numbers are reliable. They always give accurate answers. They don't change because of the way they're used. A seven is a seven. They're solid. They don't lie."

"Don't lie," he repeated. "But they can."

"Until someone with real knowledge looks at them. Then the errors are exposed. They can't be fudged for long."

More silence as they approached the center of town.

"I guess," he said slowly, "that's how you found something wrong with Ellis's books."

"Numbers don't lie," she repeated. She couldn't imagine how to adequately explain her fascination, her love of numerals.

"Do you think the loss of your parents had something to do with that? Or has someone lied to you?"

"People lie all the time," she replied, waving her hand dismissively. "Human nature, I suppose."

"Seems to be."

She decided to change the subject. She didn't need an amateur psychologist analyzing her. "Can we go to the grocery?"

"We can't cook," he reminded her.

"I can eat those veggies we bought. But you need something more and I *want* something more."

She was not at all surprised when he agreed. People could be utterly predictable in some ways. Like Hale's appetite.

THEY FOUND THE grocery down another side street. The parking lot gave it away. Tucked behind it was an older store, with none of the gleam of newer supermarkets. If this could even be called a supermarket.

Allie wandered the aisles without purchasing anything. Hale watched her, wondering what she was doing. But then she made her decision. "Let's get some sub sandwiches."

He liked that idea.

Allie loaded hers with all the veggies she could. Hale was more sparing, thinking of all the vegetables they had in the motel room. Plus, he ordered two sandwiches. When he compared the difference in how much each of them ate, he didn't know whether to consider himself a pig or her anorectic.

He had a lot more muscle to maintain, though.

"Guess we better get these back to the motel," she said. "Before they become giant icicles."

He had to smile at that. Damn, if he wasn't careful he'd develop laugh lines.

More conversations as they passed through town. Allie had an especially long one with a woman named Kerri and the two of them agreed to meet the next afternoon at the bakery for tea and cookies.

Tomorrow? Hale felt as if a noose were tightening.

Then Allie looked at him and said, "I suppose I'll have to bring you along."

Like he was going to let her out of his sight. Oh, he could imagine it, him sitting there like a hulk while two women had a tea party. Everyone was going to start wondering if he was one of those abusive guys who wouldn't let his woman do anything on her own.

That would raise their profile around here even higher. *Damn it, Allie, get real.* Or maybe she *was* being real, by her own lights anyway. He had to admit their flight couldn't have been easy on her. She'd given up everything.

He was sure, however, that she didn't want to give up her life.

Hell.

After leaving their sandwiches at the motel, they went out again. As if Allie needed to soak up every possible moment in Conard City. As if she didn't care if someone shot at her. He was going to have to make her appreciate the risk in this.

As evening began to fall, another gentle snow began to fall, as well. Allie must be getting cold, because he was sure as the devil that *he* was and he was used to this kind of weather. Growing cold had stopped bothering him a long time ago in the mountains of Afghanistan.

"Allie, this much cold exposure could give you frostbite. Or hypothermia bad enough to be hospitalized." It was also keeping her outdoors way too long.

She looked at him, a mulish expression appearing, then fading. "You're not kidding."

"No."

Slowly she nodded and turned back toward that confining, bare-bones room.

When they were back inside, stripping their outerwear, he hunted for a thermostat again. No luck. Then Allie spoke, causing him to freeze.

"You must hate me, Hale."

After a moment he turned around. "I couldn't ever hate you. But why do you think I might?"

"Because I'm being a pain in the butt. You want to keep moving and I'm keeping you stuck here. I want to be a partner in this and you just want me to follow orders."

He shook his head. The working of a woman's mind. Much more consideration than a man would show. "I am perfectly capable of putting you in that vehicle whether you like it or not. Have I done that?"

"But you're miserable. You don't like all this. Worse, you're worrying about me."

He sat on a chair to loosen his boots. "You need the break."

"Right." She sounded a bit sarcastic. "And you think I need to be protected. I guess I do. So why aren't you arguing with me?"

He shouldn't say it, but he did. "Because I like to see you happy."

Now he'd done it. He wondered what flood he'd unleashed. But she dropped the subject, turning instead to the paper plates and the vegetables she'd bought earlier. She sliced everything except the bananas into neat piles and placed it on the rickety bedside table. Then she passed out the sandwiches.

"Eat," she said. "You need it more than I do."

"After all this cold, you probably need it more than you realize."

"Can't argue with that," she said cheerfully.

"At least there's something you can't argue with."

For a while there was blessed silence in the room. No questions, no desire on his part to answer them.

Allie was affecting him and he wasn't at all sure he liked it. Something deep inside him was softening. He couldn't afford that.

The vegetables disappeared almost as fast as their sandwiches. Allie watched him take the last grapes.

"Ha!" she said. "I knew you'd like them."

"I'm not a fast-food freak."

"You're too healthy-looking to be."

He helped her clean up, then left her for a few minutes to take the detritus to the outdoor trash receptacle. There might not be any roaches he could see running around the room, but he didn't want to put out the welcome mat.

When he returned, Allie was in the shower and steam came through a crack in the door. Along with the scents of her shampoo and soap. Scents he liked.

Another curse wafted through his mind and he warned himself to cut it out. Allie could barely tolerate him, and he couldn't risk getting soft.

He wondered if he should call Stu again, then decided against it. Too many breadcrumbs. He wasn't ready to start dropping them.

When Allie emerged from the shower, towel around her head, she was wearing new pajamas she'd bought at Freitag's Mercantile. They had reindeer and Santas on them, of course.

He smothered a smile. Damn, she was something else. Tomorrow she'd probably want to get a decoration for this room. Then he looked down and saw fuzzy slippers in red and green. He hadn't noticed her picking them up.

Nor was this childish, he thought. This was a woman secure enough in herself to give in to a silly urge without apology. There was something to be said for that.

She told him again to share the bed with her. This time he did, on top of the covers. His feet had warned him, despite wool socks, how cold that floor had become.

Allie felt Hale lower himself into the bed. She was drowsy and not at all worried about it. She trusted him. He struck her as a man of honor.

But during the night, she woke to find herself cuddled in his arms. Startled, her eyes flew wide-open. What the heck?

He was snoring gently, his arms were slack. He was sound asleep. And the bedspread still served as a wall.

Her cheeks began to flush as she realized what had probably happened. Growing cold, still sleeping, she had undoubtedly sought his warmth. He was certainly radiating enough heat to warm her face and hands, even her entire body. He smelled good, too, after his shower.

Nor had he reacted to her pajamas. That made her

smile because she'd expected a glimmer of disgust. Even a small frown at the silliness. Nope.

Content and warm, she stayed where she was. Let morning bring whatever came. As sleep crept over her again, she thought, *he's damn sexy, too.*

HALE WOKE EARLY in the morning, as was his custom, while Allie still slept. He was astonished to find her curled up against him, horrified to find his arms around her.

What had he done during the night? Tried to hug her?

But he was well and truly stuck. He couldn't slide out of bed now without waking her, and she needed some sleep after the last few days.

Now he had nothing to do with his mind except try to ignore Allie's curves pressed against him while his mind wandered over a situation he'd been pondering enough to bore himself.

A mole in his group, with no way right now to figure out who it was. Yeah, maybe now he could lure the goons and the assassin into a good place for him to take care of them, but he needed Allie safely away. He'd die before he put her in worse danger despite her insistence.

She stirred a bit, slamming his mind right back into the present. Hell, he needed to get out of this bed soon. Besides, she'd probably be horrified if she found herself in this position.

Determined now, he began to ease his arm from beneath her. He achieved success at last and moved to the single chair. Allie still slept.

Well, he was capable of covert movement, he thought

sourly. This woman was crashing a lot of his beliefs about himself, however. He didn't know if he appreciated that.

God knew at what point she might decide they had a relationship.

He just shook his head and waited for her to rouse from slumber. The way she'd been going since they arrived here, she probably needed a lot more sleep.

He was beginning to long for breakfast, though. The crazy idea of leaving her here asleep and running across the way for a couple of takeouts began to dance through his mind. *Crazy* was the word for it. He wasn't going to leave her on her own until he had a truly safe place to stash her. This room wasn't it.

Needing to move, he rose and pulled on his double shoulder holster. Allie knew he had it but she'd always looked away as if she didn't approve. Or as if it reminded her they weren't playing a game. Or maybe it reminded her of her father, or Max.

Loaded, with a couple of spare clips in his pockets, he resumed his wait. Patience. He had practiced patience for many years. Why did it seem so difficult right now?

At last Allie stirred, stretching, yawning and sitting up. She gave him a hazy smile. "We're still alive?"

A dig. He accepted it. "If this is heaven, I'd rather check for another lodging."

That widened her smile. "It's so warm under these covers I don't want to get up."

But he needed her to. His stomach chose that moment to growl loudly.

Allie laughed. "I'm getting up. Must feed the lion."

She disappeared into the bathroom for a few minutes, then emerged to start quickly putting on her outerwear. "The truck stop?"

"Easiest place."

"Okay." Then she flashed him a look from the corner of her eye. "Quickest, too."

Damn, she was going to make him laugh.

AFTER ALL THE vegetables she'd stuffed in last night, Allie wasn't dismayed by the diner's menu. This morning, more trucks than ever grumbled in the parking lot and plenty of male and female truckers occupied tables. Some were available, however, and Hale once again chose seating that was away from the windows.

She wondered if he'd ever break that habit. Unlikely.

This morning she ordered fried eggs, bacon and toast. The little cups of marmalade tempted her, too.

Hale spoke after placing his own large order. "Looks like I've dragged you down to my own level of dietary misbehavior."

She smiled. "As you reminded me, it's cold out there. Besides, I filled myself with vegetables and fruit last night."

After breakfast and coffee arrived and they began eating, Hale asked, "What are your plans for today?"

"The bakery with Kerri. I'm looking forward to that. Otherwise…" She shrugged. "I'll play it by ear."

That answer had to annoy him. He was a man used to planning. Play it by ear? Did he ever do that? Or maybe he was doing that all the time, and that's what made him such a good bodyguard. After all, he was pretty much letting her have her way by staying in Conard City.

He'd hate it, but she wished she knew more about what was running around inside his head.

Then she remembered last night and how good it had felt to be curled up with him that way. It went beyond her desire for warmth. She hoped she hadn't betrayed anything else. Dang, her cheeks were flushing again. She looked down at her plate as if it were the most fascinating thing in the world.

Maybe it was. She couldn't remember the last time she'd eaten bacon so perfectly cooked.

After he'd made a good dent on his breakfast, he asked, "What are you going to do this afternoon other than meet that woman for coffee and cookies?"

"Wing it," she said again. "I love all the nice people around here. It's almost like a Christmas postcard."

"It is one."

She could almost hear the thought that must be in his mind when she said that, though his face betrayed nothing as usual. He was probably thinking that Christmas postcards were ephemeral, a thin piece of paper that could be easily torn.

A sorry way to look at life.

She wished she knew something, anything, that could make him feel cheerier. Ah, well. No chance of that, she supposed.

"What about the library?" she suggested. "Maybe I can find a book about local history."

That caused him to arch a brow. "Won't that slow you down?"

She grinned at that one. "We'll see."

SEVERAL HOURS LATER, after Allie had popped into a few shops, she looked around. Conard City *was* small, leaving little for her to explore now. Well, there was the parade tonight, but there was little else on her menu of choices for the day.

But she still refused to leave. She could, however, feel Hale growing tenser, as if he were increasingly unhappy about them lingering. Maybe he was right, but she wasn't ready to get back in that car again and drive endlessly to nowhere.

"Tomorrow is Christmas Eve," she remarked. "The children's party and gift giving. I'm looking forward to that."

There, she'd staked her claim on tomorrow, as well. If he erupted, she'd weather the storm and plant her feet more firmly.

The threat of Ellis and his minions seemed to be fading away, growing more distant. At least in her own mind. She judged Hale didn't agree. Regardless, this had to come to an end soon.

But Ellis could have given up, she reasoned. If Hale knew much about what was happening, he hadn't told her anything, which was frustrating.

"Hale? How far can we run?"

"As far as it takes."

"But how is that going to fix anything?" Not the first time she had asked.

He faced her. The street here was quiet, almost empty. Maybe most people had finished their shopping and were now at home preparing all kinds of delights for tomorrow and Christmas, for their families.

Excited kids, smiling parents, flour dusting the air as cookies and pies filled the house with delicious aromas.

She felt both wistful and envious.

"Hale?" she repeated.

He was still looking at her, as if deciding what to say, how much to tell her. Then, "We're losing some of the pursuers. Ellis's goons have dropped to a smaller number. The remainder won't quit, unfortunately, but there are fewer to deal with."

"I guess that's good."

"Considering I don't have an army, yes. That's why I've been keeping us on the move."

So something had been accomplished by all that driving. "Have they gotten closer to us?"

"Yes."

"But how?"

"When all this is over, I sure as hell am going to find out how."

She watched his jaw tighten, his eyes harden. A dangerous man indeed.

THE ENTIRE POINT of this flight had not only been to get Allie out of the immediate line of fire. It had been for him to get a bead on the pursuers so *he* could turn the tables and go after *them*.

Diminishing the number of goons had been important to his plan. Reduce their number to three or four and he could take them all out. Even better, he could question them until they squealed on Ellis.

The reduction of their numbers had at first seemed to indicate that Ellis thought he had time. That he believed

Allie hadn't gone to the authorities with her knowledge and maybe proof. That he could take care of her at his leisure.

The hired assassin had been a monkey wrench in the works. Now the diminishing number of Ellis's security people probably meant that Ellis was sure they'd find Allie. That they were growing closer to their quarry.

They'd sure been drawing closer, albeit still behind as far as he knew. He needed more adequate information about them. He wondered how to pry it out of Stu. A longer phone call would ping a tower multiple times, putting a great big X on the map, making it more dangerous when the goons were coming closer. God knew what resources Ellis had within the various phone companies.

But maybe it was time to cut line. Pull them into a trap of some kind sooner, as Allie kept insisting. He could take care of the goons but the hit man was something else. Not only would he be a sniper so he could shoot safely from a distance, but he'd also be experienced in covering his tracks before and after.

Whichever way the attack came, Allie was walking around this town like a sitting duck and didn't give a damn.

He decided it was time to call Stu again, and this time to hell with the opaque language. The threat was looming over them now, and he couldn't afford to care about eavesdroppers.

Given the way they'd been followed, he had no doubt they were drawing closer. The time was fast approaching.

He looked at Allie. "I need you to do something for me."

"What?"

"Go to the bakery and stay there until I come back. And don't sit in front of a window, okay?"

Her face paled even though her cheeks were reddened by cold. "Did something happen?"

He shook his head. "Not yet. I need to do a little scouting, and I need to know you're safe indoors with a lot of people, okay? And mind me about that window."

She nodded, her cheer deflating. "I can do that."

"Promise me, Allie."

"I promise."

"I'll walk you to the bakery before I go."

But his gaze kept straying to that church tower, looking for something, anything.

Nothing.

ALLIE MANAGED TO salvage her mood by the time Kerri arrived, escorted by a beautiful white dog with a gray face mask, like a husky. But he didn't appear to be a full husky.

"Oh, he's beautiful," she said to Kerri. Then she saw the "service dog" embroidered into his vest. "A service dog?"

Kerri nodded. "A lifesaver. You want anything from the counter? My treat."

Allie decided on a Danish and a refill on her coffee. Kerri returned with a plate full of various pastries and two coffees.

"I love this time of year," Kerri remarked. "Melinda's rarely open after noon because she's sold out."

Her dog sat beside her, watching her with adoring eyes.

"What's his name?" Allie asked.

"Snowy. Well, actually it's Snowball, but I've always called him Snowy. He doesn't seem to mind." She smiled at Allie. "Help yourself to anything. I sure can't eat it all myself. What brings you and your fiancé to this out-of-the-way place?"

"A winter holiday," Allie answered, wondering if she was about to be grilled. "We decided to meander around. I'm glad we meandered here."

Kerri grinned. "Me, too."

Placing a piece of Danish on a paper napkin, Allie broke some off. "I'm an accountant. What do you do?"

Kerri sighed. "I used to be a cop. Well, I guess I still am, of sorts."

"Used to be?"

"I got shot in the head. Epilepsy. Hence Snowy. He warns me of seizures so I don't get into trouble."

"I'm so sorry."

"I was for a while, too. I loved being a cop. But things turned around once I got here. I came to teach criminal law at the junior college. One thing led to another and I'm working as a victim counselor for the sheriff. Made me feel better." Then her eyes twinkled. "And I met my husband. Very cool."

"I should say so!"

"He's a cop, too." Kerri laughed outright. "Guess it gets into the blood in more ways than one."

"Any kids?"

Kerri spoke, a little subdued. "I'm not sure. I mean, I get these spells when I'm absolutely not aware of anything around me. How could I safely take care of a kid?"

Allie didn't know how to reply to that. It was so sad, but she didn't want to say so. Kerri appeared to be the kind of woman who'd just keep picking herself up somehow. "You're brave," she offered.

Kerri shook her head. "I'm a survivor."

"That doesn't mean you're not brave."

Kerri smiled. "Keep it up. I could get used to this."

Allie laughed.

HALE SCOUTED OUTSIDE TOWN, knowing he was probably wasting his time but needing to do so for his own peace of mind. He brought out his infrared binoculars and paused every so often to survey the wide-open expanses that surrounded the town. Not a lot of cover.

But looking through the goggles for heat signatures, he wondered if he'd see anything that looked like human passage. There were sure a lot of animals out there. Heat signatures wouldn't last long in this cold, however.

The roads into and out of town were pretty bright, though. Lots of traffic keeping them warm.

Well, that wasn't going to tell him anything. No suspiciously parked cars, either. He reckoned the assassin wouldn't arrive on foot. He needed to blend in only briefly in town, and he'd need a nearby escape vehicle. Maybe not out here, however. Parked somewhere in town, most likely.

Disgusted with his feeling of helplessness, Hale headed back into town. How the hell would this killer stick out anyway? He'd noticed that a lot of locals packed guns on their hips, and some carried hunting rifles slung over their shoulders. Hell, probably nobody would have blinked if they'd seen his twin pack.

No gun restrictions in Wyoming. Shades of the Wild West.

Hale found parking right in front of the bakery. A few people were leaving and he stood aside to let them pass, answering their smiles and greetings with a nod of his head.

Inside he saw Allie with her new friend Kerri. They seemed to be having a whale of a good time, with laughter flowing frequently.

He hated to rain on the parade but he couldn't hulk in a corner and ignore his supposed fiancée. Nope. Talk about raising a lot of gossip.

He unzipped his jacket and strode to the women, easing his way around other tables. When he reached Allie and Kerri, he did the obvious thing: he bent down and brushed a kiss on Allie's lips. The zing that zapped through him startled him. Her eyes widened.

"How you doing, darlin'?"

"We're having a wonderful time," Kerri said. "Pull up a chair and join us, Hale."

Hale could have winced. Not only had Allie revealed her own first name, but she'd apparently revealed Hale's. *X marks the spot*, he thought grimly. Don't ever assign this woman to a covert mission.

He didn't want to pull that chair over, however. First, he didn't want to talk aimlessly. Second, he was certain he'd be gently questioned about his job or whatever. What was he going to say? A lie or the truth? He hated lies.

Saving him, Kerri looked at her cell phone. "Oh my gosh, I've been having so much fun I lost track of time. We've got this faculty thing at the school tonight. I need to get ready."

The two women hugged as Kerri departed. Hale looked at Allie. "Want anything else?"

Allie was still smiling. "No thanks. Kerri kind of overwhelmed me with pastries."

He nodded and rose. "Let's go, then. I need to make a stop."

"Where?"

"You'll see."

She shook her head a little but pulled on her jacket and zipped up. Then they walked around the corner to the door of the sheriff's office.

She stopped. "Hale?"

"Yeah?"

"Has something happened?"

He shook his head. "I just want to check something out, that's all. Nothing wrong."

She didn't look as if she believed him but followed him inside. When he asked for Sheriff Dalton, he was given directions to a back office.

But first Hale looked at Allie. "Please wait here."

"But I want to know…"

"There's nothing to know. I want to describe some of the situation. Just in case. Okay?"

She nodded slowly and sat in one of the visitors' chairs, looking angry. He couldn't blame her. Then he marched down the hall.

Gage Dalton sat behind his desk wearing a dark brown winter-weight uniform. He nodded and waved Hale to a chair.

"So what's the real story?" Dalton asked before Hale could say much more than hello.

"Real story?"

"Odd couple suddenly shows up in my town claiming to be tourists on holiday and the man looks like trouble on the hoof. What's more, the two of you don't look romantic with each other. You didn't just stumble here. Or maybe you did but you've got some reason for moving around that has nothing to do with tourism."

Hale gave Dalton props. The guy didn't miss a thing.

"Well, that's what I wanted to talk with you about."

Dalton nodded. "I'm all ears."

Hale hesitated. He had plenty of good reasons for letting the sheriff know the outline, but how much detail should he provide? He began to speak, knowing there'd be questions, and not at all sure he should answer them.

"I'm not Allie's fiancé," he started. "I'm her bodyguard."

Gage Dalton sat up a little straighter, wincing as he did so. "What is she? Some kind of heiress?"

Hale shook his head. "She's an ordinary woman, an accountant who ran afoul of a very dangerous businessman as she was doing his books."

Dalton frowned. "How dangerous? Powerful?"

"Tentacles everywhere. A history of making employees disappear. Cops have been after him for years but can't get enough evidence. Anyway, Allie found something, reported it to him so he could get it fixed, and he told her *Bad things can happen*."

Gage nodded slowly. "A veiled threat?"

"Her friend, a detective that's been working this case for years, believed it was. He made her hire me and get her out of the way."

Now Gage leaned back, swiveling his chair to one side. He thought for a few minutes. "So you've got her on the run?"

"Temporarily. If she weren't so damn stubborn, we'd have been back on the road almost as soon as we got here. But she wants her Christmas, and she loves it here." He didn't mention her desire to stay here because she wanted to tighten her own noose.

"That's understandable."

"Well, I haven't dragged her out of here yet."

At that, Gage snorted. "Iron-willed."

"To say the least."

"I'm married to a woman like that. My Emma. Powerful and strong. It's made her a survivor. Okay, what more?"

Again, Hale hesitated. He wasn't accustomed to sharing a lot of detail about his operations, but he sensed in Gage Dalton a potential ally. One who probably wasn't going to like it at all when he learned the kind of threat Hale might be drawing to his jurisdiction.

"Okay," Hale said finally. "On the QT. Maybe you've heard of Jasper Ellis?"

"Some bad stuff, nothing proved."

Hale nodded. "There are several of Jasper Ellis's security goons tracking us. Worse, it appears that hard on *their* heels is a hit man Ellis hired."

Gage's face hardened when Hale spoke of a hit man. He asked, "The pro is following the goons?"

"That's my assumption, yes."

"How are they tracking you?"

Hale frowned deeply. "I suspect I have a mole in my team."

Gage swore fluently and forcefully.

"My sentiments exactly," Hale replied.

"Fire away." Gage sighed and swiveled to face him again. "You got a plan?"

"I'm trying to figure out how to draw these guys out without endangering Allie. Once I decide, I'll take them out. With interrogation, of course."

"I don't need to hear that." But one corner of Gage's mouth lifted. "I've done a little interrogation in my life. Former DEA," he added by way of explanation.

Hale nodded acknowledgment. "Anyway, I'm hoping nothing will happen while we're here. Last I heard, the goons weren't *that* close. But that's no guarantee."

Now Gage leaned forward. "You deal with it when you have to. Even here. No, I don't want the threat in my county but I also don't believe a young woman should be on the run forever when she's done nothing wrong. Trouble is, we've got a lot of fresh faces around here because of the holidays. It's not like I can pick out strangers for you."

Then Gage's eyes crinkled a bit. "You're the first legit bodyguard I've ever met. Something new under the sun."

"I don't feel new. I feel old." Hale stood. "I'll keep you posted if there's something you need to know."

"Appreciate it. And if you need any help, give me a holler." Then he added, "Got someone I can contact to verify all this?"

Hale pulled out his wallet and fished out Max's card, passing it to Gage. "Check us out with him. Careful what you say."

"I have some practice with elliptical speech."

Then Hale walked back out into the front room, where Allie was the picture of annoyance. Another small smile escaped him. Damn, that woman was a double helping of something else.

"What's going on?" Allie demanded after they stepped out into the cold again.

"Nothing you don't know." With the exception of the hired gun.

"Then why speak to the sheriff?"

Hale looked at her. "Because if hell starts raining down in this town, I want him to know we're the good guys, okay?"

She fell silent and he escorted her to the grocery, whether she wanted it or not. He kept her hand tucked firmly in his.

"Why do we want the grocery?"

"Because you're going to find something you actually *want* to eat while we warm up enough to survive tonight's festivities."

That relaxed her a bit. Probably because he wasn't threatening to put her in the car again.

One of the worst things about this, Hale thought, was

having to drag this woman all over the West and keep her as cooped up as a kidnapping victim. How much difference was there really? Only that he was trying to save her life.

He wasn't sure she appreciated it much.

ALLIE FUMED ALL the way to the grocery store. She was sick of being led around like a dog on a leash. So maybe she didn't know all the ins and outs of protecting herself, but she deserved to know what was going on, deserved better explanations. She deserved to feel more like a partner in this rather than a carry-on bag. Hell, she needed an active role, not a passive one.

"Why can't we just eat at the diner?" she demanded before they entered the store.

"Like you're a fan of diners. Load up, woman. It's going to be cold tonight while you watch the parade."

"Quit talking to me like I'm an idiot. Don't I get to choose anything?"

"So choose. Diner? Grocery?"

She could have hated him just then. Plus, she wasn't even a bit hungry and now she had to decide what to eat later?

Well, that left the damn grocery and he probably knew it. No way was she ready to order at the café or truck stop.

Most everything in a grocery needed cooking, though. That left her wandering in front of the deli counter, trying to decide which prepared foods would please her later. Preferably foods that wouldn't freeze beyond hope by the time they walked back to the motel.

She sure didn't want to load up on chips and canned beans.

The sushi looked as if it had come from somewhere else, but she picked up a package of twelve pieces. A savory chicken salad in a large container. Potato salad. Bread to make a sandwich on with the chicken salad. Then she spied smoked salmon and added that, along with some packaged bagels and cream cheese. She topped it off with some fresh broccoli and a hunk of smoked Gouda.

In all, more than enough to feed her tonight, for a midnight snack, and for breakfast. Probably enough to feed Mr. Granite, too, but she didn't have a problem when he doubled some of her choices and added a few of his own, such as cold cuts. She only wished she could make more than a couple of cups of coffee in the room. She muttered that aloud.

Hale surprised her then. He chose a cheap twelve-cup coffee maker, a container of coffee grounds and a dozen packets of dried soup. He even thought of foam cups.

Good idea, she thought acidly as she watched him. All of it was followed by paper and plastic to eat with.

Getting by must be his stock-in-trade.

She didn't feel much happier as they trudged back to the motel. Much as she loved this beautiful Christmas setting, she had to admit she was growing tired of the constant cold. A blazing fire sounded good. Even a gas fire.

No such comforts in the motel room, though. However, shortly after she stripped her outerwear, she heard the new coffeepot start to burble and the aroma of fresh coffee joined it.

Allie threw her jacket on the foot of the bed, then lay back on it. The mattress felt good and allowing her body to stretch out felt even better. She closed her eyes, then the memory of Hale's brief kiss at the bakery raced through her. Part of their role-play, she told herself. But her body didn't want to believe it.

Sighing, she rolled to her side and watched him. Best view in town, she thought with an inward giggle. He'd dumped his jacket but not his double shoulder holster. Sort of iconic, she thought. Out of a movie. Even the beard he'd been letting slowly grow back. Who was that actor who always had a two-day beard? Probably dozens of them.

Whatever, it looked good on Hale.

In fact, as much as he irritated her, Allie felt a strong and growing attraction to him. She must be losing her mind.

Stockholm syndrome, she told herself, but didn't believe it. She was *not* his captive, though she sometimes felt like it.

Sheesh. If he ever succeeded in removing the threat to her, he'd disappear back into the void of his secret world. Did she want to be left pining for the impossible?

She sighed. As if she could control her feelings.

Hale looked at her the instant she sighed. "What's wrong? I'm driving you crazy?"

"You need to ask?" She saw a furtive smile touch his mouth. He was becoming less stony as time passed.

That might be even more dangerous than the man she had originally met.

The *zap* she felt when their eyes locked ran through her entire body. She closed them at once, shielding herself. As if she could. Long-ignored desires fluttered hotly inside her, making her core pound in time to her heartbeat.

An overwhelming wish that he'd come over and begin seducing her wouldn't leave her alone. A chicken's response, she argued with herself. Putting herself at the mercy of Hale's decision. She ought to have more gumption than that.

Except she didn't need his rejection right now. On top of the way her life had been torn apart, she didn't know if she could handle it. Strong as she'd been trying to be, stubborn as she'd insisted when she could, she felt as if the remains of her life might shatter.

But of course he wouldn't approach her. If nothing else, he'd believe it to be a violation of trust. If there was one thing she was sure about, it was that Hale was an honorable man.

The yearning still thrummed in her anyway. She had to hope Hale hadn't read it on her face in those few moments. Had to hope she hadn't embarrassed herself.

But she was still a young woman with healthy needs and while she didn't give in to them often, this time the need was almost overwhelming.

God, he was sexy. Sexier than any man should be. Yet he let no one close. No one. Even the few times he'd opened up to her, while they gave her a snapshot of his internal life, he didn't reveal much. Didn't she have to know a man better than this?

Her body didn't think so.

Then she felt the edge of the bed dip beside her. Startled, she opened her eyes again and found Hale sitting beside her.

"Allie? There are a million reasons I shouldn't touch you."

"Yeah," she said a bit sharply. "Naturally. Hale Scribner, the man who won't let anyone close. God forbid a mere woman should penetrate your armor."

"Hell, you're not a *mere* woman. I've told you things I've never told anyone else."

"So. Just save your precious isolation and go away."

Quite to the contrary, he leaned over her, caught her chin gently in his hand and turned her face upward so he could kiss her. No light brushing, but a strong, determined kiss.

"Allie," he breathed, "I want you. I want all your fire, all your stubbornness, all your fear and bravery. You take my breath away."

She wanted a snappy comeback, but it wasn't there. Instead her arm, as if it had a mind of its own, reached up to wrap around his powerful shoulders.

"Are you sure?" he asked against her lips, his breath a warm whisper.

"Yes." A quiet reply.

"Then I'd better get rid of this holster."

And more than that, she thought, her mind hazy through her deepening desire. But by the time he did that, he'd have plenty of opportunity to change his mind. She tried to steel herself.

Except he didn't change his mind. He not only got rid of his double holster, but he got rid of every stitch of clothing until he stood in all his naked magnificence in the golden light of the room's only lamp.

Just as she'd seen him come out of the shower that night, only now without a towel. Every one of those toned muscles was dangerous, but she didn't care. He'd taken care of her this long, he would continue to.

"I'm going to make you cold," he said quietly, then started removing all her clothes. Carefully. Pausing to take time to brush over her nipples, her waist, then the secret between her legs.

Cold? She felt like a flaming torch. She wanted no delay. She needed culmination. To feel him deep inside her, filling an empty space that demanded it. Needed it.

But he continued to take his time until even her socks were gone. Then he kissed the arch of each foot, moving upward to kiss her inner thighs, to drop kisses on her belly. When he reached her breasts, he licked them and sucked on her nipples.

He was driving her out of her mind.

She clutched for his shoulders, trying to drag him closer. She wanted his weight on top of her, surrounding her.

Then he answered her wish, cloaking her in the heat from his body, capturing her face between his hands.

"You're perfect," he murmured. "Absolutely perfect. Beautiful. More beautiful because of how drowsy you look right now."

She was more interested in the rigidity of his staff pressing against her belly and her private parts. So stiff, so ready, so large, like the rest of him. More thrills ran through her, and never had she felt so worshipped.

He moved against her, tantalizing her, not yet entering her as if he wanted to drive her to insanity first. She was coming close.

"Hale," she murmured huskily. "Hale, please…"

He answered her plea, entering her slowly. Gently. With each deepening of his penetration she felt herself expanding, the most delicious sensation ever.

Then he was all the way in and he reached down between them, rubbing the nub of her need even as he began to move.

She felt as if she were caught on a welder's arc, so hot, so needy.

But before long his movements sped up and she felt as if she were riding a whirlwind of hunger. Higher and higher until satisfaction claimed her in a thunderclap of ecstasy.

He wasn't far behind. With one final thrust, he shuddered and reached his own pinnacle.

She drifted down like a feather on a gentle breeze.

HALE PULLED THE bedspread over them and cuddled her in a warm cocoon. His hand ran up and down her side, almost like petting.

"I'll have to go back on duty soon," he offered quietly.

"I know." This departure from the norm might have been risky. At least he would think so.

"I'd like to stay right here with you all night," he answered huskily. "But I can't. We're already running enough of a risk staying in one spot for so long."

"Then why haven't you dragged me away?"

"Because you're stubborn. Because I want you to have your Christmas."

His answer pierced her heart with warmth. He'd cared enough about that to run a risk. Maybe a huge risk. Would he never stop surprising her?

"Still want to go to that parade?" he asked her as he finished dressing.

"No," she answered, surprising herself. "I'd like to sit here with you and eat our grocery stash. What I'd really like, if we can, is to go see the Christmas party for the kids tomorrow."

He hesitated before answering. "I need to make a call first, find out how we stand. Okay?"

"It had better be good," she answered saucily.

This time a genuine smile crossed his face. He headed out the door.

She rolled around in the covers for a few minutes, then put on her flannel nightgown. It was becoming her favorite.

Surprising her, Hale stuck his head in the door. "I need to take a short walk. Keep the door locked."

"How short a walk?"

"Fifteen, maybe twenty minutes, okay?"

"But why?"

"I'll tell you when I get back."

She guessed she had to be satisfied with that.

Besides, it would give her time to hug herself and

enjoy the afterglow he'd left in her. Her mind ran over his each and every touch as if trying to etch the entire experience permanently in her mind.

Man, sex had never been so good.

Chapter Thirteen

Outside in the frigid air, Hale retrieved another of his phones. He had a good supply of them but the pile was still shrinking. Without inserting the battery, he stuffed it into one of his inside pockets.

After he closed the tailgate, he checked the packed snow that currently obscured most of the license plate. Good enough. Considering the weather they'd been having around here, it wouldn't even look suspicious.

Then he set out on a hike toward the center of town. He dipped into the Mercantile, spent a few minutes and some of his own money, then came out with a small bag tucked in his pocket. The parade was moving down the street with plenty of noise, so he sought a quieter place to make the phone call.

"Stu."

"Yeah," came the familiar voice. "My cats got out and are now heading west. At least it looks like. You sure you don't have some catnip?"

"I don't believe so."

"Then check again, good buddy. I don't know where that catnip is, but the change in direction…"

Hale understood completely. Someone had picked up on something somewhere. For all he knew they were following a map of stolen license plates. Which shouldn't bring them directly here. And he knew for sure he hadn't revealed his current location to Stu.

The fact that Stu didn't have his location made him doubt he had a leak in his team. Then what?

He tossed the dead phone and chip on trucks headed in different directions, then crossed the highway to the motel.

He didn't enter immediately, however. He had some mulling to do and Allie's presence wouldn't make it any easier.

How closely were they being followed? So far he'd say not. But they were being *successfully* followed. Damn it, *how?*

Could his use of those pay-per-use phones really be tracked? Could a single ping on a tower be getting noticed?

Given Ellis's resources, he wouldn't be surprised. That meant they could be pinged here. He could have turned the air blue with curses but he didn't want to draw any attention.

He should get Allie out of here right away. Except he wasn't sure staying was a problem and he wasn't sure if his phones were the problem and Allie had made her position clear. She wasn't going to move without a damn good reason, especially since she didn't like being *baggage*. She was impatient with the whole idea that he could catch these guys without exposing her.

One more day, he told himself. He could keep her safe until after the Christmas party and then they were going to hit the road again.

One more day. He could do it. He didn't want to take the happiness from her any sooner than he must.

One more day, he promised himself yet again. He'd just have to stay on extraordinarily high alert. No different from Afghanistan.

Although Allie had locked the door from the inside, he was able to use his key to open it. Another security breach he ought to consider dealing with.

Much to his amazement, when he entered he discovered she'd laid out all their food on paper plates for dinner.

"Five-star service," he remarked as he shed his jacket.

"Well, I had to do something to fill the time. Dig in. I'm going to." She promptly proved it by popping a piece of cheese in her mouth. "It's pretty good, too, although I'm a little afraid of the sushi. I'm sure it wasn't made here."

"Honestly, I'm surprised you found any at all." He paused, then added, "You didn't miss much of a parade. Santa riding a sled on the back of a pickup truck with a couple of mechanical reindeer. Oh, and Santa was tossing candy canes to the kids. The most I can say about it was that the Christmas music piped over speakers was deafening."

Allie laughed. "Charming. But you're right, I'm not sorry I missed it."

"Oh, yeah, don't forget the police car leading the

front and the fire truck bringing up the rear. Dang horns were like to make my ears scream."

They ate in silence for a while, even the sushi, which they decided was edible if not great.

But then Allie had to bring it up again. "What did your friend say?"

Well, he didn't have an honest answer to that, so he tried to find a hedge that wouldn't be lying. "They're still looking. No pinpoint yet."

"That's a good thing, right?"

"Yeah." As long as he was getting the full information. The skin on the back of his neck began crawling again.

Something was seriously wrong. But he'd have to face these guys sooner rather than later because Allie couldn't spend the rest of her life on the run. She'd made that very clear, including running an incredible risk by planting herself here. But he wanted it to happen at the place of his own time and choosing, with Allie safe whether she liked it or not.

He needed better info. More than the general direction they were heading. Stu was giving him the best information he could, or so it seemed, yet the noose appeared to be tightening anyway.

Hell. There'd been times in Afghanistan when he'd wanted to crawl out of his own skin because the air had been filled with threats he couldn't see.

This was one of those times. Bad enough to have those goons on Allie's tail, but a paid assassin? What the hell had Allie discovered? Could she even explain it to him in a way he'd understand? Not that he needed to. All that mattered was the danger to her.

Maybe it was time to call Max and see if his web was tingling at all. Except he didn't want to call Max and possibly draw him into this mess. Max's phone might even be tapped, hence his warning to the sheriff.

All he could say at this point was that taking Allie on the run had reduced the number of pursuers to a manageable group. It wouldn't matter, though, if he couldn't corral them and put an end to this chase.

He cleaned up the detritus of their supper, hauling the trash out to the bin at the end of the hotel. His eyes were never still, scanning for any movement, anything out of place. If those goons were in the truck parking lot, however, he'd never be able to pick them out.

Not unless they acted oddly. He watched for a few, then got his butt back to Allie. At least if anyone tried to break in he could stuff her under the bed and take out the threat.

It should only be so easy.

The goons probably didn't have murder on their agenda. That would be more people than Ellis would want to know his plans.

But the pro seriously worried Hale. Nothing would stop him even if he had to chase Allie to the ends of the earth.

Allie spoke. "You're getting uneasy." Then wistfully she said, "I guess you don't want to stay for the kids' party tomorrow."

He looked into her hopeful face and hated what he was doing to her. "It's at noon, right?"

She nodded.

"Then we'll go afterward." A few hours. He doubted they'd make much of a difference now. If he drew the danger into this town, so be it. He'd scoped the place enough to know where the risks lay.

But he was settling into his mission mindset, the one that had kept him alive in the most threatening situations. Now he needed it for Allie.

Because he was long past caring what happened to him.

ALLIE WAS DISAPPOINTED when Hale didn't come to bed with her. She so longed for a repeat of last night.

But she'd also come to know him well enough to realize he was getting wound as tight as a spring.

She closed her eyes, dealing with her own selfishness. Becoming difficult, wanting her Christmas. All of it was causing him serious strain. He hadn't dragged her all over the place, driving her for miles through one small town to another because he *wanted* to. He'd probably enjoyed it no more than she had.

But he was devoted to protecting her and she was making it so much more difficult by demanding to be part of what he was doing. God, she wasn't one to stand by, especially when she thought her own pigheadedness was the only way they would ever deal with this.

But why hadn't he just insisted that she get in the car? Why hadn't he physically dragged her to get on their way? Why had he let her set herself up? Did he privately agree that hers was the only way to get at the pursuers? Didn't sound like Hale to her.

She could only conclude that he'd judged the threat to be far enough away to make it possible to stay for a few days.

But whatever his judgment had been, she wasn't immune to realizing he was turning into honed steel again.

Chapter Fourteen

In the wee hours, while Allie slept the deep sleep of the innocent, Hale reached a point where he could barely stand it anymore. He'd pushed this mess to the breaking point and his internal alerts had begun to sound like a Klaxon.

Allie's demand that she take an active role in this didn't help his mood any. He damn well had to find out more about their pursuers.

Stepping outside, just beyond the door, he pulled out another of his phones and stared up at the starry sky. The morning would arrive brilliant with sunlight. That might help.

Then, stepping away from the door, he called Stu again. Stu sounded a bit sleepy.

"What the hell?" Hale demanded.

"I was hoping you'd call," Stu said. "Damn phones you're using, I can't call *you*."

"News?"

"Two more cats have changed direction, leaving only two together. You *must* have catnip."

"I'd like to find it. Lay it on."

"Would you recognize any meaning for two horse-shoes tipped on their sides in the same direction?"

Hale didn't have to think. Conard City. Or Conard County. Either one was bad enough. His heart beat more heavily, but more slowly. The adrenaline was just beginning to course through him. "Why do you ask?"

Stu paused a minute. "You know how I told you I was thinking my house is haunted? Nobody's been around to move my decorations. So, I got a ghost and he's been banging around since last evening and tipping my horseshoes. Know an exorcist I can get fast? Like immediately?"

Hale didn't answer. He and Allie had been pinged somehow. Okay, then. And the ghost had to be Casper, only a few hours east of here. He closed his eyes tightly before speaking again.

"Sprinkle some holy water," he said finally. "I'll let you know about the exorcist if I can find one."

He ripped the phone apart, knowing it was now a useless safety measure. How the hell were they being tracked?

Only one thought occurred to him. He opened the tailgate and looked inside his box of phones. At the very bottom he found one that contained both SIM card and battery.

He wasn't stupid enough to have done that. Someone had gotten into his phones. He picked up the one he had just used and called Stu again.

"Yeah?" Stu answered.

"Somebody screwed with one of the phones. Find him."

Then he disconnected, threw the phone on the ground and ground it beneath his heel.

The game was on. Except that it was no game.

And now he had to tell Allie the whole sorry story.

HE MADE A pot of coffee and used the smaller motel pot to boil water for the packaged soup. Then he woke Allie as gently as he could.

She stirred slowly from a deep sleep. As soon as she sat up, still groggy, he put a foam cup of chicken soup in her hands.

"What's happening?" she asked.

"A whole helluva lot. Swallow that soup. We need to talk."

That seemed to wake her instantly. She set the soup on a bedside table and pulled the bedspread up to wrap around herself. "Shoot."

"I told you I was trying to lose as many of Ellis's security people as I could."

She nodded, reaching for the soup. "Yeah. Because you're not an army."

"Well, they've been cut to two."

She reached for the cup and sipped the soup slowly. He was sure it wasn't too hot because that little pot didn't keep the water hot for long. "That's good news, right?"

"To a point."

She wrapped both hands around the cup, sipping more. "What's going on, Hale? Just finally tell me the truth about what you're doing. Tell me the real dimensions of this threat that has you so worried. I'm tired of being kept in the dark, and tired of being treated as if I can't deal with anything."

She'd been trying one way or another to make that clear to him since her initial shock and disbelief had worn off. He'd watched her impatience grow until she had finally dug in her heels and said she was tired of being treated like luggage.

He hadn't meant to make her feel that way, but his focus had been entirely on keeping her safe. He should have listened better.

"I wish you didn't feel that way," he said.

"I'm a woman. I'm *used* to being treated that way. I've never liked it."

Ah, hell, now he was a misogynist? "I don't think women are stupid or are little girls. I've fought beside enough of your sex to know better."

She smiled with satisfaction, then drained the last of her soup. "So treat me like one of those women you fought beside. Fill me in on the mission."

But how to find the right words? He had to choose, starting with the smallest parts. Then would come the paid killer, and she wasn't going to like that part at all.

"Okay, we're down to two goons on our tail."

"Manageable for you, I'd bet."

"Most definitely. More soup?" He needed the pause to choose his words carefully.

"Why do I have the feeling this is going to be a cold morning? Since we're filling me with hot liquids, bring me some coffee and get yourself some. It can wait that long or you'd have already thrown me over your shoulder and jammed me in the car."

He kept his lips zipped while he made her more soup, then poured coffee for each of them. So she'd imagined him doing the caveman thing. "I won't say I haven't thought about it."

She snickered. "I would never have dreamed."

He felt a corner of his mouth twitch in response as he ferried cups to the bedside table. No, hang on to his iciness. Don't let himself soften.

She helped herself to the coffee first, blowing on it gently. "Spill," she said.

No escaping it any longer. He wasn't looking forward to reading her reaction on her face. He'd become fond of the cheerful woman she'd turned into in this town.

"Okay. Two goons. Minimal threat. We winnowed them out good, Allie."

"Well, you did most of it."

"And you came along for the ride."

She looked down and smiled. "Being generous there, Mr. Tough Guy. Better take it easy."

But none of this was going to be easy. None. He sighed.

"All right. They're headed here. Directly here, according to my source. They left Casper just a little while ago, and they evidently know where we are. My source sure figured it out somehow."

She looked at him, reflecting dismay. "How? How do they know? I saw all the precautions you took."

"Honest to God, I really don't know for certain. What I *do* know is that my team managed to get tracers on all their vehicles. I've been watching their numbers fall away, but maybe that means they found a way to keep tabs on us and didn't need as many goons."

"But how?"

He shook his head. "I found a phone in my stash that was still hooked into the network. Somebody must have done that."

"A betrayer?"

"I'm worried about that. But I'm also sure that might not explain it."

She asked for another cup of coffee. "Then I have to put myself in plain sight. I'm sure they won't grab me from the town square."

"Probably not." Now came the difficult part. Now he *had* to tell her. He steeled himself against her probable reaction.

"So here's the thing," he said after a delay to drink coffee. "The thing I haven't told you. The thing that's kept us moving so fast. Those goons by themselves weren't a big enough threat."

He heard her draw a sharp breath. She quickly put aside her coffee and wrapped her hands together. "What is?" she asked quietly.

He fired the words like bullets. "A professional hit man."

Her face paled until it was almost white. The reaction he had feared. Probably to be followed by sheer terror.

She sat frozen for a minute, maybe longer. Finally she shook herself and whispered, "He'd go that far?"

"Ellis is a dangerous man. Max and I have emphasized that enough."

"But why a professional?"

"Because he'll never talk. Because he'll vanish into the woodwork the minute his job is complete." Hale drew a deep breath of his own. "And he *will not quit* until he finishes the job."

"Oh my God..." The words barely emerged from her throat.

"This *is* the rest of your life, Allie, unless I stop him."

She nodded jerkily, still pale. She twisted her hands but he could still see them shaking. He could do nothing to prevent it, nothing to reassure her. And there was more to come.

She looked at him, searching his face. "You always looked hard, Hale, but not as hard as you do right now."

"Mission face," he answered, although that was probably an understatement given the feelings for her that he was burying in a crypt inside his soul.

She drank more coffee. He waited as if for the guillotine. He wouldn't blame her if she erupted like a volcano, or melted into hopeless, frightened tears.

She held out her cup. "Give me a few minutes, please."

Well, that was a calm response. So far. He poured them both more coffee and returned to waiting. She had to absorb this, but a time clock had begun to tick in his head.

She spoke, her voice steady. "A sniper?"

"I think so. Trying to get up close and personal would just get messy."

"God, a sniper." A shudder ran through her. "I thought that happened only in movies."

"I wish."

She drank some more coffee. "They're deadly. Always accurate."

"Usually."

Her eyes had grown hollow. "Usually?"

"Depends. This one is at a disadvantage. No spotter to calculate a trajectory for him. So he'll have to move in closer."

She nodded. "How close?"

"The range of a decent deer rifle."

"That's still a long way."

"It changes my calculations," he said flatly. "He's got only a few lines of sight in this town. And he sure as hell can't shoot much over a hundred yards around here, which narrows the area I have to watch considerably."

"So maybe if I just keep moving…"

Now the rest of the bad news. "Unlike in the movies, you can't move faster than a bullet. No one can."

Her hand shook once, then she finished the coffee and put the cup down with a quiet thump. "That's it, then. I have to be visible or he'll never take a shot at me. He'll just keep coming."

He'd been fearing this from the outset. Trying to scramble together a way to avoid exposing her. But he couldn't just wander around out there hoping to spy a guy who'd probably blend in like one blade of grass in a lawn. That was another thing these snipers were good at: being invisible in their surroundings.

He spewed a few good cuss words. "I'm messing up my job. I've been trying to think of a way to avoid this, to get the sniper without exposing you, but we couldn't get him painted."

"Painted?"

"We don't know where he is. We couldn't get a bead on him. He's out there somewhere is all we know."

She pursed her lips. "Wouldn't he be with the goons?"

"I figure he's following them. They don't know about him."

"Why not?"

"Because Ellis wouldn't want them to know. The more people who know, the more people he has to get rid of. They probably think they've been sent to convince you to keep your mouth shut. Maybe to offer you a lot of money to walk away. But Ellis wants more than a deal."

"I guess so." She frowned thoughtfully. "So how do we handle this? I need to be in the open, and you can't get to him if you don't know where he is."

"You're absolute sure about doing this? Think about it, Allie."

She nodded. "I'm sure. My dad wouldn't have run."

Well, that settled it, he decided grimly.

"I've scoped the town. I know his likely spots. I'll keep an eye on them. But before it gets light, you're going to come with me to the sheriff's office. You won't like wearing body armor."

Now she looked astonished. "Body armor?"

"You better believe it. I'm not going to have you out there walking around like an oblivious deer. The armor will be heavy, but it'll protect you against anything a hunting rifle can shoot."

WELL, THAT WAS some comfort, she thought. Her insides twisted but she wasn't going to quit. Hell no. She'd been arguing that she wanted to be a partner in this, and now was her chance.

"I can take you out of here," he offered as they donned their clothing.

"No." She wasn't surprised he'd offered, but she'd had enough. Maybe all this was making her suicidal or something, but it had to stop. At any risk.

Her spine had stiffened to the point that it felt rigid. All of her was tightened up, but it was now or never, as they said.

Hale drove them to the sheriff's office. It was still dark, but dawn was beginning to gray the eastern horizon.

"Is he already out there?" she asked.

"Most likely, if the goons are convinced you're here then the shooter has been informed by his employer. Which means he's already found a hiding place. But he won't shoot until the light is good enough and you're in the right place."

"Can't we search for him?"

"Not enough time now. I'd have to look too many places. So I'll keep an eye peeled for any unusual movement at any elevation, the higher the better for his purposes."

"There are a lot of upper-story windows out there," she remarked as a shiver ran through her.

No kidding, he thought as he rolled them into a parking space. "Don't stop, just head for the sheriff's door."

He watched her dart inside, then headed for his bank of phones. No point in the usual precautions now. He called Stu again.

"Yo."

"Stu. We're getting ready to take on the problem. What I need from you is a paint job. Keep an eye on the cats. I'll call."

"You got it."

Then Hale stuffed the phone in his pocket and headed inside. To his surprise, Gage was already there.

"You get up early," Hale remarked.

"I'm addicted. Actually, most of my nights are disturbed. Old injury. No point in bothering Emma with my pacing around the house."

Hale nodded. The sheriff had already installed Allie in a chair.

"Don't drink the coffee here," Gage said. "Battery acid. All those bottles of antacid are there for a reason."

"I take the warning."

"Fill me in," Gage said, leaning back against the edge of a desk. A couple of deputies manned other desks and were trying not to look too interested.

"I have reason to believe the pro may already be in town. He probably hid himself overnight."

Gage nodded. "Great. Okay. What do you need me to do?"

"Give Allie some body armor. She's going to be standing in the square being a target."

"Damn! You want me to send some uniforms out to look around?"

Hale shook his head. "Anything changes, he'll skedaddle faster than a cat. Then we gotta look again."

Gage turned to Allie. "You up with this?"

"Now or later," she answered steadily. "I'm choosing my ground."

Damn, she was one hell of a woman. Courageous. Hale tipped her the slightest smile.

Gage spoke again to Hale. "You want armor, too?"

"No. It'd slow me down."

"I'm sure I have some gear that will fit Allie," Gage said as he headed down the hall. "This is some Christmas Eve."

ALLIE NEEDED HELP with the armor. Hale knew the ins and outs. The main thing she noticed was the weight. Heavy stuff. Hanging from her shoulders. Riding up her neck like the world's worst turtleneck. As if that wasn't enough, the sheriff handed over some arm protection and thigh protection.

"Gotta protect those arteries." Dalton walked around as Hale helped her into her jacket. "It has a hood. Good."

Then he went to a locker and handed Hale a dark helmet. "This should fit under her hood."

"God," Allie said when they'd finished dumping weight on her. "My knees are going to hate me."

Hale shrugged. "Sit in the snow if you need to. Or on a bench. At this point…"

"What I *can* do," Gage said, "is make sure some of my folks are wandering in the park with her. If we all keep moving, it might take him longer to sight on her."

Hale nodded. "Good idea. I wasn't going to ask that anyone take a risk."

"You didn't ask. Give me a few and we're going to have some apparently ordinary citizens walking around the square, not too far from Allie. Maybe in a friendly group around her."

"At least I'm warm now," Allie remarked. Then she dropped onto the nearest chair.

Allie knew now the weight and discomfort of this body armor, and she felt the greatest admiration for anyone who could wear it and function. They probably trained with it, but still.

It was also hot, particularly under her outer clothing. Well, she sure wasn't going to get cold this morning.

Hale stopped her before they exited. "Allie, swear to me you're sure about this. It's flying in the face of everything I do."

"You know, Hale, if this is the kind of danger you protect people from, you deserve a lot more than I'm paying you. I'm sure. I'm done. This is no life."

She was determined, but also afraid. Even with the armor. *Nobody can outrun a bullet.* Dear God.

People were already gathering in the square, in a conversational knot. They greeted her like a friend and drew her in with them. Hale came along but his eyes never held still. He had drawn down his balaclava, becoming white from head to ankle. Blending with the snow.

Allie kept looking at him. He hadn't said it, but he'd be a target, too. The thought of never seeing him again scared her more than getting killed herself.

She was pleased to see that Kerri was there with her dog. A couple of the others she recognized from her conversations around town. They were all cops?

But now they were dressed in regular winter clothing. Were they wearing armor, too? She hoped so. She didn't want anyone else getting hurt because of her.

One of the men, tall and lean, spoke to Hale. "I'm Seth Hardin. Retired SEAL. You need anything from me, let me know."

"Thanks. I gotta stroll around. Keep your eye out for any unusual movement from above. Oh, and I may need your help chasing a couple of cats. Need to bring them in."

"Will do."

Hale eased away from the group, sure that the sniper would have to wait until the crowd spread out a bit. Breathing room. But not much.

He tried to look as if he were just wandering while he kept scanning elevations from second story up. Higher if the pro was farther away.

He hoped the balaclava made him unrecognizable if the pro knew who he was. Which had become more likely than not.

ALLIE'S NERVES STRETCHED tighter and she wondered if they would snap. Standing here with these brave people wasn't making her feel any braver.

The guy had to take his shot before he disappeared again. Had to. And Hale had to take him down.

She spoke. "I'm going to step away briefly. He's got to be able to start aiming."

Six faces eyed her with concern. Then the one called Seth nodded. "But don't move too far away. Don't make it too easy on him."

"I won't. Can't you tell I'm scared as the devil?"

Seth smiled. "You're hiding it pretty well. Welcome to the reality of courage."

"Meaning?"

"Courage isn't being unafraid. It's doing the dangerous thing *despite* the fear."

"I'd guess you'd know. All of you." She drew a deep breath. "Here I go."

Just a few steps, she assured herself. She doubted she could do any more than that in this damn armor anyway.

HALE COULD HAVE exploded when he saw what Allie was doing. He didn't know whether to admire her or get furious. Didn't matter. Right then he was filling with enough adrenaline that he was nearly past feeling anything at all.

He performed another quick scan, then saw a small, brief flash of light from the bell tower on the church. The rifle scope had caught just enough light to reflect it. Careless.

But it was the carelessness he needed. Adrenaline took over completely and he started running, unzipping and pulling a pistol from his left holster. Less than two hundred yards. A walk in the park. Seeing him, the sniper might already be packing up.

Reaching the church, Hale wrenched open the door and, still running, he headed for the spiral staircase. His own breaths sounded loud in his ears. Then he heard a gunshot from above. The sniper had picked out his target from the group.

Allie. God, Allie. His vision turned red with rage. Nothing could stop him now.

Get him. Get him. The words pounded as hard as his heart.

He tore open the door to the staircase and began running upward because there was no point in trying to be quiet. The guy had already taken his shot. He wouldn't be able to use his rifle on these narrow winding steps, walled on either side.

The hit man was now on the run but with nowhere to go. Because of the narrow stairway, the guy was probably waiting above in the bell ringers room, ready to shoot whoever was coming.

Hale knew one thing. If he opened the door above from the hinge side, the creep wouldn't be able to see him immediately. It should give Hale just enough time to get off the first shots.

IN THE SQUARE, Allie felt a punch in her chest. The pro had fired and the armor had protected her. She felt her knees start to shake. Would he fire again? Maybe she *should* collapse, pretending to be shot. Her throat clogged with terror as she waited for the next bullet.

PISTOL AT THE READY, Hale encountered the man in the bell ringers room, just as he'd anticipated. The man had his own pistol in his hand. At this point, the guy apparently didn't care about leaving tracks.

Hale didn't hesitate. He fired six shots in rapid succession. Center mass. The guy stumbled and fell, the pistol falling from his grip. The amount of blood that began pouring down the stairs told him the man was dead or would be in less than a minute.

He considered another shot to be sure, then waited. At last he was certain. Eliminated.

Allie heard the shots, amplified by the bell tower, and now did collapse onto the snow. She was immediately surrounded.

"Hale," she whispered. "Hale."

"I'm going," Seth said. Then he raced off in the same direction.

HALE STOOD AT the foot of the stairs, phone in hand, when Seth reached him. "Arrest me for murder. Later."

"Forget about it, man. What now?"

"Making a call. There are two goons out there and my contact better know exactly where."

"Yo," Stu answered the phone immediately.

"The exorcist is gone. Now give me the acolytes. You painted them?"

"Bright red. Ready?"

Hale looked at Seth. "I'm going to repeat some coordinates."

Seth nodded and took out his own satellite phone. "Shoot."

A few minutes later, he and Seth headed out in vehicles in slightly different directions. Hale didn't waste time checking on Allie or reassuring her. It was enough that he saw her and she saw him.

And he still *had* to collect the two security guards.

Chapter Fifteen

An hour later, stripped of body armor and surrounded by her group of friends in the sheriff's office, friends who had risked their lives for her, she drank coffee that a deputy had brought from Maude's.

Hot, foamy, a perfect latte. Except she could hardly taste it. It was over, or almost so. She felt as if she might dissolve with relief. But she kept shaking. A reaction perhaps.

Hale must be okay, she reasoned. She'd seen him run with Seth to the vehicles out front. Both of them spun tires as they sped away.

They must be after the goons Hale had spoken about. The ones he wanted to question. The last bit. If they revealed enough, Ellis would be taken down. That should be enough to make her safe.

If she could ever feel safe again.

At last, Hale and Seth Hardin came through the door with two zip-cuffed men. Dalton was awaiting them.

Gage asked Hale, "You want to question them now or later?"

"Can you hold them for me? The questioning might

take a while and I want to feed Allie, then take her to our room so she can unwind."

Gage nodded. "I can hold them, alright. Got two miserable jail cells upstairs. Maybe we'll start with stalking. I'm sure I'll be able to add more crimes. It appears six people saw someone shoot at Allie, so forget any charges against you. We'll find more."

"Like one of those goons taking a shot at Hale," Seth Hardin said. "Stupid move."

Hale squatted in front of Allie. "Let's go to Maude's. Or you can wait in the car while I get takeout. Either way, after all that adrenaline, we both need to eat."

Allie's only desire was to fall into his arms. The room sounded more inviting, but he was right about food. Especially for him.

"Takeout," was all she said.

"I GOT YOU a salad and a club sandwich," Hale said coaxingly. "Please try something, Allie. You have no idea how much energy you burned up this morning. I don't want you to get sick."

"In a minute," she answered. Her voice trembled and she sat on the edge of the bed without even pulling off her outerwear. "I'll be okay in a minute."

"I know you will. You're tough."

Then he sat down beside her and put his arm around her shoulders. He reached for the zipper on her jacket and pulled it down. "You're going to be hot soon. Let's get you out of some of this."

She didn't resist, even helped by standing up and

tugging herself. At last she was in jeans, a sweatshirt and her socks, then sat on the bed again.

Hale rose, stripping his own jacket and snow pants, as well as his double holster.

"Look," he said, "I got us some lattes. Let's drink them before they get cold."

She accepted one, and realized she was coming back from the brink of the breakdown. Steadily returning to normal. "That was harrowing," she said, her voice stronger. "God, a movie has nothing on that."

"Not when it's real," he agreed. "Not when you're the one standing out there knowing you're a target."

"I was more worried about you," she told him flatly. "I was all covered up with armor and helped by friends. You were out there chasing a madman all by yourself."

"Nothing I haven't done before."

Her gaze finally lifted to his. "I know it isn't. How you could do it repeatedly is beyond me."

"Youth and belief in one's immortality."

At last she felt a smile begin on her lips. "That wasn't your excuse today." But she let the subject go as he insisted on bringing out the container with the club sandwich in it.

"Did your man find the traitor?"

"Yeah, he did. He told me when I called after taking down the goon. Guy's name is Dan. And he's been the reason our intelligence was so spotty."

"God, you must feel so betrayed."

He did, but Stu would handle that. Right then, Hale had more pressing concerns.

"Eat just a little," he said, placing the open container

on the bedside table. Then he turned, reaching for the jacket he'd thrown over the chair, and pulled out a small crumpled paper bag. He returned to sit beside her.

"I know it isn't Christmas yet," he said huskily. "And I'm not in the habit of doing this, so call me awkward. But I bought you a Christmas present."

She gave a weak laugh, then took the bag from him. Opening it, she found a small black velvet box. Her breath caught. "Hale?"

"No big deal," he said. "The Mercantile isn't exactly overloaded with good stuff. But I thought you'd like this."

She took the box in both hands, then opened it slowly. Again her breath caught. Inside was a silver butterfly, a small delicate one, on a silver chain. "It's beautiful," she breathed.

"The real thing, too. Not rhinestones."

"It wouldn't matter," she said honestly. "What a fabulous necklace! You're a surprising man, Hale Scribner."

"Yeah, I know I'm not the type, but I can learn."

Putting the velvet box aside, she twisted and threw her arms around him. "Thank you! Thank you!"

Somewhere between her first thank-you and her second, they wound up lying on the bed, face-to-face, tightly embracing.

"Your sandwich will get stale."

"Hang the sandwich," she answered, pulling him closer for a deep kiss. "I want you more."

Epilogue

Two days later, days of wondrous lovemaking as far as Allie was concerned, Hale was content that he'd pried all the information he could from the two goons. He'd passed it all along to Max, promising the Conard County Sheriff's Department would be transferring them. Max sounded like he was over the moon, at least as much as a hard-boiled detective could be.

Allie spoke with Max for a while, even telling him about the armor and being shot at, but she concluded with the highest praise for Hale.

He felt embarrassed.

Then Max said, "Don't come back yet. I need to make sure this end is wrapped up tightly enough to protect Allie. And Allie? Do me a favor and don't get stubborn. Ellis doesn't quit easily."

Allie looked at Hale after she disconnected. "My life is still at risk? For heaven's sake!"

"Only briefly," he promised her. "We've got enough to take him down along with any cooperating henchmen. Once that's done, anyone remaining will be too afraid to continue this hunt. They'll see the cost."

"I hope you're right."

"I'm always right."

That pulled a laugh from her. "You're something else, Hale Scribner."

"I never lied to you. Anyway, I wouldn't mind a week or two here in your Christmas wonderland. It'll give us time to know each other better."

She pursed her lips. "Why would we want to do that, Mr. Tight Lips?"

It was his turn to smile. "How many names do you have for me?"

"Quite a few. Most of this trip I've had nothing better to do than think them up. You still haven't answered my question."

"Because," he answered slowly, as if to be sure she heard every word, "despite all my attempts to remain detached, I haven't succeeded. You're a fascinating, charming, stubborn thorn in my side. And oddly enough, Ms. Amazing, I think I'm slipping into love with you."

Allie caught her breath, her eyes widening. When she recovered her breath, she said, "Make it a fast slide, Hale. Because I'm already in love with you."

He hugged her close, as if he wanted never to let go. "Trust me, it's not going to take long. I'm mostly there. Now, want to take a walk through this over-Christmased place?"

She beamed. "I'll go anywhere with you."

"Almost," he corrected, then kissed her deeply.

"A new life," she murmured against his lips. "I think I'm going to like it."

* * * * *

"If need be, I could run my way out of these woods. You can't
run," Linnea added.

"No, but I can return fire if we get into trouble," Jace argued.
"And I stand a better chance of hitting a target than you do."

It was a good argument. Well, it would have been if he
hadn't had the gunshot wound. It wasn't on his shooting arm,
thank goodness, but he was weak, and any movement could
cause that wound to open up.

"You could bleed out before I get you out of these woods,"
Linnea reminded him. "Besides, I'm not sure you can shoot,
much less shoot straight. You can't even stand up without help."

As if to prove her wrong, he picked up his gun from the
nightstand and straightened his posture, pulling back his
shoulders.

And what little color he had drained from his face.

Cursing him and their situation, she dragged a chair closer
to the window and had him sit down.

"The main road isn't that far, only about a mile," she
continued. Linnea tried to tamp down her argumentative tone.
"I can get there on the ATV and call for help. Your deputies and

the EMTs can figure out the best way to get you to a hospital."

That was the part of her plan that worked. What she didn't feel comfortable about was leaving Jace alone while she got to the main road. Definitely not ideal, but they didn't have any other workable solutions.

Of course, this option wouldn't work until the lightning stopped. She could get through the wind and rain, but if she got struck by lightning or a tree falling from a strike, it could be fatal. First to her, and then to Jace, since he'd be stuck here in the cabin.

He looked up at her, his color a little better now, and his eyes were hard and intense. "I can't let you take a risk like that. Gideon could ambush you."

"That's true," she admitted. "But the alternative is for us to wait here. Maybe for days until you're strong enough to ride out with me. That might not be wise since I suspect you need antibiotics for your wound before an infection starts brewing."

His jaw tightened, and even though he'd had plenty trouble standing, Jace got up. This time he didn't stagger, but she did notice the white-knuckle grip he had on his gun. "We'll see how I feel once the storm has passed."

In other words, he would insist on going with her. Linnea sighed. Obviously, Jace had a mile-wide stubborn streak and was planning on dismissing her *one workable option*.

"If you're hungry, there's some canned soup in the cabinet," she said, shifting the subject.

Jace didn't respond to that. However, he did step in front of her as if to shield her. And he lifted his gun.

"Get down," Jace ordered. "Someone's out there."

Don't miss
Pursued by the Sheriff
by Delores Fossen, available January 2022 wherever
Harlequin Intrigue books and ebooks are sold.

Harlequin.com

HIEXP1221

*Amina Kelly may be divorced, but she wouldn't
want her ex dead. When her ex is killed on duty,
Maxwell Layton comes back into her life—and the
passion between them is just as strong as ever. Now they
have to fix their past mistakes—while dodging someone
intent on making sure Amina doesn't get out alive...*

*Read on for a sneak preview of
His to Defend,
the latest thrilling romance from Sharon C. Cooper!*

"All of that's true and I hate this has happened to you,"
Maxwell said. "But you've forgotten one important fact.
You weren't harmed. At least not physically. Everything
in that house can be replaced."

"That might be true, but—"

"But you—" he kissed the side of her forehead
"—sweetheart, you're irreplaceable, and I'm glad you
weren't hurt. Now, *that*? That would've made the evening
a helluva lot worse. Because if that had happened, I
would be out for blood. We wouldn't be sitting here
together because I'd be out hunting that bastard. Instead,
we have others looking into the situation while you and I
are getting ready to try to salvage our date. So how about
we start by enjoying an excellent meal?"

After a long beat of silence, Amina sighed dramatically and leaned back to look up at him. A slow smile tugged the corners of her lips. "Well, when you put it that way, I guess I should pick a restaurant, huh?"

He grinned and handed her the menus. "Yes, and I'll take the bags upstairs, then change clothes. When I come back down, we can order." He stood and headed for the stairs again but stopped when she called him. "Yeah?"

"Thanks for coming to the house. It meant a lot to have you there with me even though I know it was the last place you wanted to be."

He studied her for a moment. "That might've been the case at first, but I want to be wherever you are, Amina. And I'll always be here, there or wherever for you. Remember that."

Don't miss
His to Defend *by Sharon C. Cooper,*
available January 2022 wherever
Harlequin Romantic Suspense
books and ebooks are sold.

Harlequin.com